DEMON WALK

BOOK 6 OF THE LACEY FITZPATRICK AND SAM FIRECLOUD MYSTERY SERIES

MELISSA BOWERSOCK

NEW MOON PUBLISHING

Copyright © 2017 by Melissa Bowersock

All rights reserved. No part of this book may be reproduced, stored in a retrieval system or transmitted in any form or by any means without the prior written permission of the publishers, except by a reviewer who may quote brief passages in an online review or one printed in a newspaper, magazine or journal.

First Printing

All characters appearing in this work are fictitious. Any resemblance to real persons, living or dead, is purely coincidental.

Cover image by coversbydesign.net.

ISBN-13: 978-1978479043
ISBN-10: 1978479042

ACKNOWLEDGMENTS

I have to start out with an apology. I believe it is the author's job to be as authentic as possible while still crafting the best story possible; sometimes those two goals conflict. In the case of this book, I'm afraid I have played fast and loose with the layout of Mission San Juan Capistrano and the surrounding area, and for that I apologize. However, my tweaks were necessary for the story, and for that I do not waver. I hope, rather than look for inconsistencies, the reader will simply sink into the story and enjoy it. I certainly did.

Books by Melissa Bowersock

The Appaloosa Connection
The Blue Crystal
Burning Through
The Field Where I Died
Finding Travis
(No Time for Travis Series Book 1)
Being Travis
(No Time for Travis Series Book 2)
Fleischerhaus
Ghost Walk
(Lacey Fitzpatrick and Sam Firecloud Mystery Book 1)
Skin Walk
(Lacey Fitzpatrick and Sam Firecloud Mystery Book 2)
Star Walk
(Lacey Fitzpatrick and Sam Firecloud Mystery Book 3)
Dream Walk
(Lacey Fitzpatrick and Sam Firecloud Mystery Book 4)
Dragon Walk
(Lacey Fitzpatrick and Sam Firecloud Mystery Book 5)
Demon Walk
(Lacey Fitzpatrick and Sam Firecloud Mystery Book 6)

Soul Walk
(Lacey Fitzpatrick and Sam Firecloud Mystery Book 7)
Blood Walk
(Lacey Fitzpatrick and Sam Firecloud Mystery Book 8)
Castle Walk
(Lacey Fitzpatrick and Sam Firecloud Mystery Book 9)
Murder Walk
(Lacey Fitzpatrick and Sam Firecloud Mystery Book 10)
Spirit Walk
(Lacey Fitzpatrick and Sam Firecloud Mystery Book 11)
Fire Walk
(Lacey Fitzpatrick and Sam Firecloud Mystery Book 12)
Revenge Walk
(Lacey Fitzpatrick and Sam Firecloud Mystery Book 13)
Gangster Walk
(Lacey Fitzpatrick and Sam Firecloud Mystery Book 14)
Karma Walk
(Lacey Fitzpatrick and Sam Firecloud Mystery Book 15)
Mystery Walk
(Lacey Fitzpatrick and Sam Firecloud Mystery Book 16)

Bordello Walk
(Lacey Fitzpatrick and Sam Firecloud Mystery Book 17)
Storm Walk
(Lacey Fitzpatrick and Sam Firecloud Mystery Book 18)
Predator Walk
(Lacey Fitzpatrick and Sam Firecloud Mystery Book 19)
Prayer Walk
(Lacey Fitzpatrick and Sam Firecloud Mystery Book 20)
Mind Walk
(Lacey Fitzpatrick and Sam Firecloud Mystery Book 21)
Deception Walk
(Lacey Fitzpatrick and Sam Firecloud Mystery Book 22)
Innocent Walk
(Lacey Fitzpatrick and Sam Firecloud Mystery Book 23)
Monster Walk
(Lacey Fitzpatrick and Sam Firecloud Mystery Book 24)
Dead Sea Walk
(Lacey Fitzpatrick and Sam Firecloud Mystery Book 25)
Heart Walk
(Lacey Fitzpatrick and Sam Firecloud Mystery Book 26)

Night Walk
(Lacey Fitzpatrick and Sam Firecloud Mystery Book 27)
Stone Walk
(Lacey Fitzpatrick and Sam Firecloud Mystery Book 28)
Execution Walk
(Lacey Fitzpatrick and Sam Firecloud Mystery Book 29)
Suicide Walk
(Lacey Fitzpatrick and Sam Firecloud Mystery Book 30)
Twilight Walk
(Lacey Fitzpatrick and Sam Firecloud Mystery Book 31)
Redemption Walk
(Lacey Fitzpatrick and Sam Firecloud Mystery Book 32)
Hopi Walk
(Lacey Fitzpatrick and Sam Firecloud Mystery Book 33)
Healing Walk
(Lacey Fitzpatrick and Sam Firecloud Mystery Book 34)
Trojan Walk
(Lacey Fitzpatrick and Sam Firecloud Mystery Book 35)
Betrayal Walk
(Lacey Fitzpatrick and Sam Firecloud Mystery Book 36)
Goddess Rising

Lightning Strikes
Love's Savage Armpit by Amber Flame
(Originally published as
The Pits of Passion)
The Man in the Black Hat
Marcia Gates: Angel of Bataan
Queen's Gold
The Rare Breed
Remember Me
Sonnets for Heidi
Stone's Ghost
Superstition Gold

DEMON WALK

Melissa Bowersock

ONE

"So, Sam, tell our viewers how you do what you do. How do you communicate with ghosts?"

Glen Stamos, the square-jawed host of the *Glen and Holly Morning Show*, smiled at Sam expectantly. The petite Holly Fraser, beside him on the couch, leaned forward with wide-eyed interest.

"It's, uh, hard to explain," Sam said. "I think it's different for everyone with mediumistic abilities, but for me, it's a matter of focus and concentration. I just block out as much sensory input as possible and tune into the ethereal sensations. It's a little like blocking out the sound and picture of a TV right next to me, and concentrating instead on a faint radio playing down the hall in another room."

Lacey watched her Navajo partner with sympathy. He hated this—the questions, the attention, the hype. His extraordinary talents, second nature to him, were an unknowable superpower to the show hosts—

and their viewers—and intensely interesting. What he did naturally, instinctively, they saw as some weird aberration, spiritual mumbo-jumbo, or outright fabrication. They examined him as they might an exotic bug.

"What about you, Lacey?" Holly asked. "Do you feel things like Sam does?"

"Oh, no," Lacey said, happy to take the spotlight off of Sam for a minute. "I'm afraid I don't have any of Sam's ability like that. I rely on research and my own analysis. Hunches, really. We come at an investigation from completely different perspectives, but we always meet up at the end."

"And get your man," Holly added, alluding to their success in tracking down murderers.

"Or woman," Glen joked, arching an eyebrow at his co-host.

Lacey smiled painfully at the byplay. Was everything a joke to these people? Did everything have to be cute? It was enough to make her gag.

"Don't go away," Glen said to the camera, "because after this glimpse into private investigators Sam Firecloud and Lacey Fitzpatrick, we're going to take a look at everything pumpkin spice, and later… ballroom dancing! Stay with us."

By the time Sam and Lacey made their way out of the TV station into the bright sunlight, they were both just grateful to be done.

"Holy crap," Sam said under his breath. "Can we not do anything like that ever again?"

Lacey managed a rueful laugh. "I think next time we get an invitation to go on TV, we'll have to watch the show a few times before we decide. That was just painful."

"Tell me again why we have to do TV at all," Sam grumbled. He took his phone out of his pocket and turned it on, checking for messages as they walked to the parking lot.

"Because," Lacey repeated for the umpteenth time, "it builds credibility and lets people know we are for real. The more familiar people are with our work, the more likely they are to call us, and the more likely *we* are to catch the bad guys."

He wasn't listening. He had his phone to his ear. Lacey gave up. Maybe they wouldn't do any more TV. She actually wasn't sure it was worth it.

She pulled her keys from her purse and unlocked her Toyota.

"Hey," Sam said, holding up his phone. "We got a call. The director of San Juan Capistrano."

Lacey blinked at him. "The mission?"

"I guess." He climbed into the passenger seat. "Let me call him back and see what he wants."

Lacey put her key into the ignition but didn't start the car. *See,* she wanted to say to Sam. *People call us. That's a good thing.*

"Mr. Swayze? This is Sam Firecloud. I got your message…"

Sam listened for a moment, then interrupted. "Excuse me, sir. Let me put you on speaker so my partner can hear you, too." He punched a button and said, "Okay, go ahead."

"As I was saying," the little voice said, "we're having a problem with a particular area of our grounds, and we think it's something you could help us with. There's no, uh, normal explanation for it. And it's getting worse."

"All right," Sam said. "When would you like us to come down and have a look around?"

"Tomorrow too soon?" the director asked hopefully.

Sam looked at Lacey. She was already nodding.

"Sure. What time?"

"How about ten a.m.?"

"We can do that," Sam said.

"Good." The director let out a relieved breath. "Here's the address…"

Sam grabbed Lacey's notebook from the console and scribbled the address.

"Got it," he said. "Okay, we'll see you tomorrow."

"Thank God," the man murmured.

Sam hung up the phone and glanced at Lacey. "Don't say it," he cautioned.

"Say what?" Lacey asked innocently.

Sam hooked a thumb at the TV station behind them. "He saw us on the morning show. Called as soon as the segment was over."

"Oh." Lacey stifled a laugh and started the car. "Whatever you say, boss."

Maybe it was worth it after all.

~~~

Melissa Bowersock

TWO

    Rocketing down the I-5 toward San Juan Capistrano, Lacey appreciated the straight shot and one-hour drive. So often in Southern California, a trip of any distance involved one or two or three interchanges, jumping from one freeway to another. This was a breeze.
    Sam's phone pinged. He didn't answer it.
    "No one you know?" she asked.
    "No. I tell you, Lacey, I'm getting just crazy stuff. One guy left me a message asking if I could give him the winning lottery numbers. Just nuts."
    "Blurgh," she huffed. "This really is a two-edged sword. Like I've been saying, our fifteen minutes of fame can help people reach us for very real problems, but on the other hand, we get the wackos, too." She looked over at Sam. "I'm sorry. I didn't think about that."
    "Eh." He shrugged. "It's not your fault." He grinned wickedly. "It's Captain Shaw's fault. He's the one who started this with that

press conference and those awards he gave us."

Lacey laughed. "True enough. But it was really sweet of him to recognize us for our work on that last case. Believe me, he doesn't give out attaboys easily. Even when I was still a cop, he did not hand out praise lightly. And for him to recognize us as private investigators, well, that's a milestone."

"Yeah, I get that. And I'm glad you're getting the recognition you deserve. Me, not so much."

Lacey reached over and squeezed his hand. "Thank God for voicemail, huh?"

"Yeah." He squeezed back. "And caller ID." He slipped his phone into his pocket. "Here's our exit," he said, pointing.

"Got it," she said. She put on her blinker and steered down the offramp.

The city of San Juan Capistrano was just slightly schizophrenic. The style of the old adobe and stone buildings of the mission carried over to the new buildings: whitewashed walls and red tile roofs. But all around the perimeter of the mission grounds were crowded chain stores and fast-food outlets: Starbucks, McDonald's, Chili's. The mission, enclosed by its protective walls, was an island of religious history in a sea of modern commercialism.

They found the parking lot nearest the administration building and piled out of the car. Taking a walkway to the front door, Lacey noticed the overriding sense of peace here: the gardens, the ponds, the swaying palm trees and the pastel fuchsia and salmon flowers of the bougainvillea. *This would be a nice place to come to every day*, she thought.

Inside, signs steered them to the director's office. They entered the open reception area and walked to the woman behind a counter.

"May I help you?" the woman asked. Fortyish and trim with short, dark hair, she stood to greet them.

"I'm Lacey Fitzpatrick and this is Sam Firecloud. We have an appointment with the director at ten a.m."

"Oh, yes, of course. How do you do? I'm Belinda Armstrong." She offered her hand to each of them over the counter. "Let me check to make sure he's ready for you. Would you like some coffee or water?"

"None for me thanks," Lacey said. Sam shook his head as well. Belinda excused herself and slipped through the door behind her.

The office was tastefully done. White walls and Saltillo tile harkened back to the colonial Spanish origins of the mission and the town that grew up around it. Only a single picture graced one wall, a stunning sunset behind the Basilica, bathing the graceful domed building in pink and orange light. A small arched niche in the opposite wall held an unadorned bronze crucifix.

Lacey turned to Sam. "Anything yet?" she asked.

Sam grimaced. "The original mission is over two hundred years old," he said quietly. "There are plenty of ghosts here."

"Oh." She hadn't thought of that. "Will it be hard to cut through the noise?" she asked.

"I should be able to, but we'll have to wait and see."

Just then Belinda's heels tapped out her return. "Director Swayze will see you now." She motioned them toward the open door.

"Thank you," Lacey said. She preceded Sam into the office.

Nice digs, she thought. A high-ceilinged room with clean white paint, two windows set into the thick walls. Bright area rugs scattered over the tile, bookshelves across one entire wall. The morning breeze through the windows brought the cool, dry air of fall.

"Hello," Swayze said as he rose from his chair. "Come in. So nice to meet you."

They all shook hands, and Swayze motioned them to red leather chairs with nailhead trim.

"Thank you for coming," he said. "We really were out of options, so when I saw you two on TV yesterday…" He shrugged and pointed skyward. "It seemed like a sign."

Sam and Lacey exchanged a quick, startled look.

"I'm, uh, not sure you want to describe us as heaven-sent," she said. "We're just private investigators."

"Ah, but very special private investigators. Am I right?" Swayze smiled at them.

Sam managed a crooked smile. "Let's just say not your average, garden-variety type."

"Exactly," Swayze said, pleased. "So how do we do this?"

"First off," Sam said, "what's the area that has the problem? I'd prefer to walk it before you tell me much about what people are experiencing. I'd like to get my own impressions before I hear yours."

"Yes, of course," the director said. "Here, let me grab a brochure." He pulled a tri-fold brochure from his desk and laid it open on the surface.

"Here's a map of the grounds. As you can see, most of the mission property is bounded by commercial properties all along Camino Capistrano to the west. On the east, across El Camino Real, are schools and other businesses. It's not until you go to the northern end of the property that you see residential neighborhoods. It's this area that's the problem."

Sam studied the map. "The entire northern end?"

Swayze looked slightly uncomfortable. "The northeast corner, actually. Here." He pointed to a very specific spot.

Lacey watched Sam peruse the map. She wasn't sure, but she had a feeling he was already picking up something.

"As I said, I don't want a full-blown description now, but can you give me a sense of the nature of the problem in just a few words?" Sam asked.

Swayze sat back in his chair and steepled his fingers. "Oh, I can give it to you with one word."

They waited.

"Evil."

~~~

THREE

"Evil," Sam repeated.

Swayze nodded. "I don't know if you folks are religious, but I'm guessing, in your work, you've come up against evil a time or two."

Sam cleared his throat. "I'm Navajo, so my spiritual path is slightly different..."

"But still," Swayze said. "In your Navajo belief system, does evil exist?"

Sam stared at him, his face expressionless.

The director stared back.

"Yes," Sam said finally. "It does."

Swayze spread his hands as if to say, *there you go.* "Well," he said, "let's get you out there and you can see for yourself." He keyed an intercom. "Belinda, would you ask Father David to come in?"

"Yes, sir."

"Father David will escort you out there. He's in charge of the Mission Basilica School, which is closest to the problem area. And, when you're ready, he can tell you what some people have experienced." He folded up the brochure and offered it to Sam. "Want to keep this?"

"Yes," Sam said. He took it and stuck it in his back pocket.

A knock sounded on the door, which then pushed open. A tall priest with thinning hair came in. He was dressed all in black except for the small white section of his collar. Swayze made the introductions.

"This is Father David Ruiz. Lacey Fitzpatrick and Sam Firecloud."

Lacey and Sam stood and shook hands. Lacey noted the man's gentle grip and his rather sad, dark brown eyes.

"Our guests here," Swayze told Ruiz, "want to see our 'problem area.' Sam has requested that we don't tell him anything about what's occurred out there until he's seen it for himself." The director turned to Sam. "I'm assuming you'll ask questions as you're ready to hear more."

"Yes," Sam said.

"All right. Take as much time as you need, and I'd appreciate it if you'd all come back here when you're done, let me know what you find."

"Certainly," Lacey said. She smiled to Father David. "Lead the way."

Outside, the peaceful solitude of the mission was pierced by children's calls and shouts floating on the breeze from a school across the street.

"Is that school part of the mission?" Lacey asked.

"No. That is the unified school district. Our schools are here on the property."

"So there are a lot of children about," Lacey said. Children in close proximity to an evil presence? That did not bode well.

"Yes, there are," Father David said. He met Lacey's eyes for a moment, and she could see the worry there.

She knew she was right.

They neared the far northeast corner of the property. Lacey deliberately slowed her pace, falling behind Sam, and she noticed that Father David stayed with her. She dug quietly in her pack for her phone and set it on video. She wanted to be ready for anything.

Suddenly Sam slowed as well. Lacey put out her arm, motioning Father David to stay back, and started filming.

Sam's steps slowed even more, but at the same time his body tensed. Lacey noticed he pulled himself up to his full height, and thrust his chest out. She'd never seen this attitude, this… defiance in him.

Wondering what it was that evoked this response made the skin on her arms crawl.

She swallowed down her trepidation and kept filming.

Sam came to a halt. He was facing almost due north, but then Lacey saw him look to his left, to the west. He held his body stiffly, head up, as if testing the air. After a brief moment, he swung his head to the right, and went completely still. Lacey studied him through the screen of her phone. She saw no movement in his body, no rise and fall of his chest, no change in his facial expression. It was as if he'd been turned to stone.

That's stupid, she thought. But she continued to look for movement—the twitch of a facial muscle, a blink, anything—to prove he was alive. After what seemed like several long minutes, she finally saw the set of his shoulders move, as if he were loosening tight muscles. He turned due east, toward the street beyond the wall. Then he began to slowly back away.

When he drew near to Lacey and Father David, he sucked in a deep breath and turned to the priest. His eyes were wide, and had an alarm in them that Lacey had never seen before.

"You see," Father David said. It was not a question. "You feel it."

Sam nodded slowly. He pointed to the eastern wall. "It comes from over there."

"Yes," the priest said. "And it's getting stronger."

"Do you know where it originates?" Sam asked.

Father David turned and began to walk back, but not to the admin building. Instead, he walked that way a short bit, then angled toward the wall. Sam and Lacey followed.

At a gate in the wall, he stopped. He pointed over the wooden gate.

"You see those houses over there?" he asked.

Sam and Lacey looked where he pointed. The beginning of a residential neighborhood, older houses, but well-kept. It didn't look like anyone's version of a "problem area," Lacey thought. She turned back to Father David.

"Do you see that first house, the white one with blue shutters?"

Lacey nodded.

"Now see that small house tucked back behind it?"

"That's a house?" Lacey asked. She squinted at the flat-roofed building, thinking it looked more like an old adobe shed than a house. The area around it was bare ground with a few weeds, nothing that spoke of care of even habitation. The two windows were small and dark.

Both Lacey and Sam looked to the priest for an explanation.

"That house is very old, as you can tell," he said. "The woman who lives there has owned it for decades. She will not sell it. Even as newer, larger homes were being built all around it, she won't let go." Father David sighed. "We believe the... presence issues from that house."

Sam stared at the unremarkable little building, then scanned the area on either side. "Does the feeling radiate out in all directions?" he asked.

"We believe so," Father David said. "We aren't completely sure. Some of the people in this area refuse to even talk about it, or admit it exists. As if, maybe giving voice to it makes it real. They ignore it, probably hoping it will go away." He paused. "It doesn't."

"How long has it been like this?" Lacey asked.

The priest turned and started walking back toward the director's office, and Sam and Lacey fell in beside him.

"As long as anyone can remember. There have been rumors, legends, for years. Sometimes there seems to be more activity, sometimes less. Or maybe it's a matter of more reports. I don't know. It's so easy to dismiss uncomfortable feelings, you know?"

"But the experiences you're having now?" Sam asked. "What's been reported?"

The priest looked distinctly uneasy. "Many of the staff here won't even venture to that back corner. The facilities manager has problems getting maintenance people to work out there. They report feeling that they're being watched, even stalked. Some report having difficulty breathing. We had a boy not long ago say he felt like he was being choked."

"Any witnesses?" Sam asked.

"Actually, yes. He was with three other boys, playing hide 'n' seek. The other boys saw him stumble out of his hiding place behind a tree, his hands at his throat as if he were trying to pull something off. He was crying, coughing, gagging, until he managed to run back toward the center of the campus. Then he felt he could breathe again."

"Any marks on him?"

"Not then, not right away, but the next day he had bruises. As you can imagine, his parents were very upset. There was quite a row about it in the director's office. The parents insisted the bruises had to come from another student, maybe even from a teacher, but the boy held to his story. Even so, the parents pulled him out of our school." The priest shrugged. "I don't blame them."

As they neared the administration building, they were all thoughtful.

"And you say it's growing," Sam said. "Growing in size—in scope—or in strength?"

Father David shot him a worried glance. "Both."

They filed into the building and Belinda waved them into the director's office. Swayze was on a call but finished up quickly, hung up the phone and leaned on his desk. Lacey started her recorder.

"What do you think?" he asked.

Sam didn't mince words. "You have a problem." The director's shoulders slumped. It was obviously not the response he'd been hoping for.

"We'll have to do more research to find out exactly what it is and where it comes from"—Sam glanced at Lacey—"but it's definitely threatening. I felt like a black cloud was looming over me out there—dark, oppressive... dangerous. And it was more difficult to breathe out there. Almost like heavy, humid air. And it got more difficult to breathe the longer I was out there."

Sam looked down at the floor for a moment, gathering his thoughts. "Normally," he said, piecing it together, "very few spirits attempt to make contact directly. They are usually bound up in their own anguish, and they relive it over and over like a loop. If their agony is very strong, it bleeds over to the living people close by, who may see things, hear things, feel things. But the contact is more accidental than deliberate."

He paused. Lacey was glad the director didn't press him, but let him sort it out at his own pace.

"There have been times when spirits have reached out to me," Sam continued. "When they've asked my help to release them." He shook his head. "This thing doesn't want help. It wants to kill. And it's not terribly particular about who its victims are."

The room was silent. Lacey felt a distinct chill, although the morning sunlight outside the windows looked as bright and warm as ever. She chafed the skin of one arm with her hand.

"So what you're saying," Swayze paraphrased, "is that this will just continue to get worse?"

Sam nodded. "Worse, in every way possible."

The director and Father David exchanged looks. The priest turned to Sam. "That was my assessment as well, even though I don't share your ability. If someone should die here at the mission, a child in our care..." He swallowed. "Well, obviously, that would be unconscionable. What can we do to get rid of this thing?"

Sam studied the priest's face as he considered the question. "I'm afraid I don't know exactly—not yet, anyway. I need to find out more about it, who it is, what its history is. Why it is the way it is." He glanced around the room, noting a crucifix on the wall. "Has anyone tried exorcising it?"

Swayze sat back in his chair, seeming to distance himself from the very idea. Father David looked uncomfortable.

"I did," he said. Swayze's eyes widened. "I went out early one morning, before anyone else was here, and I sprinkled holy water on the wall. I began to recite the Lord's Prayer, but when I got to the part about deliverance from evil, I felt it… roar at me. Not in voice, not in sound at all, but in feeling. As if it were charging me, leaping at me. I, uh, I'm afraid I faltered and ran."

Sam listened sympathetically. "That's about what I would expect," he said. Father David looked only slightly mollified. "This thing is old. I believe its power comes from ancient wisdom, ancient magic, magic drawn from the very earth itself. I'm afraid modern religions can't defend against it."

The director ran a hand through his close-cropped hair, frustration evident in his face. "So what do we do? We can't sacrifice a chicken out here." He waved toward the wall.

Sam smiled grimly. "Let us work on it. What's the address of that house over there? And what's the name of the owner?"

Lacey immediately dug out her notebook and a pen from her pack, ready for the details.

Father David gave her the address. "The woman's name is Pilar Archuleta. She's very old, lived there all her life. She speaks very little English. I know she has family; sometimes I see a car over there, and a young woman takes her shopping. But that's all I know."

Lacey wrote the information down, then waited for Sam's direction. This was one case where she was completely in over her head.

"All right," Sam said. "Let us work on it." He stood up, and Lacey followed. The other men scrambled to their feet.

"So that's all?" Swayze asked, obviously frustrated.

Sam leveled a look at him. "For now, yes. I can't go at this thing blind. It's too powerful. I need to know what I'm up against."

"All right." Swayze settled somewhat. "I think I understand. But you'll keep us informed?"

Sam nodded. Lacey pulled out cards and handed them to the director and the priest.

"We'll call you with our progress, or if we have any questions," she said. "But if you—or anyone here—thinks of anything that might be helpful, don't hesitate to call."

They all shook hands. Father David gave Sam's hand a heartfelt squeeze. "Thank you," he said with obvious relief. "We were totally out of options."

"Don't thank me, yet," Sam said wryly. "But we'll do all we can."

He and Lacey left the two men staring thoughtfully after them.

~~~

FOUR

Lacey was glad to get out into the sunshine again. The autumn warmth helped to chase away the chill that had gripped her.

She headed for the car. "So I'll get right on property records…" She stopped when she realized Sam was angling off toward the east. "Where are you going?" she asked.

"Come on," he said, waving her along. "I just want to walk over that way."

Surprised and not particularly pleased about it, Lacey followed him down the driveway to the street. "I thought you said you didn't want to go at it blind," she muttered.

"I don't." He held out a hand to her. "Trust me?"

She took his hand and let him pull her across the street. "Of course. But if you were trying to scare those guys back there, you did a pretty good job. Did a good job on me, too."

He smiled at her grimly. "Don't worry. I just want to push against the bubble a little.

See how much resistance there is. I'm not ready for a full-on confrontation yet."

Lacey felt only slightly better about that.

They gained the sidewalk on the opposite side of the street and Sam released her hand. She settled her day pack more firmly on her shoulder and kept pace with him as they approached the residential area. Sam walked briskly until they neared the property line of the little adobe house. Then he motioned for Lacey to stop behind him.

"Stay there," he said. "Just give me a minute."

Not liking this at all, Lacey pulled out her phone and began to video.

Sam approached the mostly bare ground where it butted up against the sidewalk. He stopped there, peering into the property, scanning the empty yard around the house. He kept his hands free, his arms loose, but he held his body stiffly upright.

Lacey zoomed in on his face. He wasn't unfocusing his eyes as he often did when he walked. His stare was fully aware, fully cognizant of his surroundings. His nostrils flared. She'd never seen him hold himself apart from a spirit they were investigating, but perhaps they'd never encountered one like this.

Suddenly he raised his hand—and waved! Waved toward the little house.

Lacey could hardly believe what she was seeing. He smiled. Smiled and nodded, then turned and walked back to her.

She clicked off her phone and tossed it in her day pack. "What was that all about? Who were you waving to?"

He touched her elbow and guided her across the street. "The old lady in the house. She saw me through the window and waved to me. So I waved back."

Lacey stared at him.

"Watch the sidewalk," he said. She glanced down and saw they were nearing the curb, and if he hadn't said anything, she would have tripped. "And close your mouth; you'll catch flies."

"But, but..." Lacey's mind churned with all sorts of questions. She did her best to untangle them. "So you don't think that she...?"

"She's the source? No, I don't." They headed back onto the mission grounds toward the parking lot. "The entity, I'm pretty sure, is male. At least it feels like male energy. I'm not sure what her relationship is to it, but I felt like she recognized me as... a helper. Someone sympathetic."

"That's a good thing," Lacey grumbled. "From the sounds of it, we need all the help we can get for this." She locked eyes with

Sam over the roof of the car as she opened her door. "Have you ever run into anything like this?"

Sam shook his head. "Not like this, no," he said, sliding into the car. "You remember the witch we came up against out on the reservation?"

"As if I could forget," Lacey muttered. The Navajo witch—a shapeshifter—had been the weirdest case she'd ever worked on. It was also the first time she'd ever felt stalked, and in real danger, since pairing up with Sam.

"This is worse," he said. He put his hand on her shoulder and squeezed. The reassuring touch was belied by the serious look in his dark eyes. "We're going to have to be very careful with this."

She nodded, swallowing down a feeling of dread.

~~~

FIVE

As soon as she got back to her apartment, Lacey jumped on the computer to begin her research. Property records were an easy way to start.

Pilar Archuleta had owned the property since 1949. Before that was Humberto Casales, since 1918. Before that... nothing.

Lacey started to dig. She searched on Pilar's name and found her mentioned in an obituary... for Humberto Casales.

Humberto Maria Casales left this world on July 6, 1949. Born September 27, 1890, to Octavia and Guillermo Casales, he was instilled with an abiding love for the Lord, and served that love his entire life. He was schooled at the Mission San Juan Capistrano and attended divinity school in San Diego. Upon attaining the priesthood, he returned to San Juan Capistrano as a humble servant and conscientious teacher. He guided with love and compassion, helping many of his young students find their own true path to the Lord. He will be remembered for his gentle soul and pure heart.

Humberto was predeceased by his parents, two brothers and a sister, as well as his wife, Ramona. *Funny*, Lacey thought. He was a priest but he was married. Maybe back then, the rules were more lax, or maybe it was a common law sort of thing. At any rate, Lacey skipped past the names until she found Pilar's, listed as his firstborn child. There was no mention of a cause of death.

Lacey jotted down notes as she put the timeline together in her mind. So Pilar inherited the property from her father. Lacey thought that was fairly unusual for a woman in a Hispanic family of that time, but perhaps it made sense because she was the oldest child. Interesting that the family was so firmly rooted in the area—and the mission. She wondered if neither Director Swayze nor Father David mentioned the connection because they didn't know it, or didn't think it pertinent. She made a note to herself to check.

Humberto bought the property in 1918, when he was approximately twenty-eight years old. Young to become a property owner, especially on a priest's small income. Lacey remembered Father David saying rumors and legends about the evil presence had been reported for decades. If the evil was known as far back as 1918, would Humberto have bought the property? That would seem rather foolhardy. Yet Pilar had been there for decades and refused to sell or move away. Why would anyone choose to live with a presence like that? Especially if she didn't share the evil nature, as Sam suspected.

The names and dates only told her so much. She went back to her search results and found Pilar again, this time mentioned in an obituary for her husband, Manuel. He had died in 1958. If Pilar had become the homeowner after her father's death, it struck Lacey as odd that her husband would not have been listed as a co-owner, since they were married at that time. They married in… she scanned the article… 1937. That was eighty years ago. Lacey sat up.

How the hell old was Pilar?

Quickly she accessed birth records, confident that Pilar was born in California. She knew her parents' names, so…

Bingo. Pilar Henrietta Casales, born to Humberto and Ramona Casales… in 1916.

Jesus, Lacey thought. *She's a hundred and one years old.*

A hundred and one years old and living in close proximity with a demon ghost? What was up with that?

This case just got weirder and weirder.

Lacey pushed her laptop away and stood up, stretching her legs. She walked to the sliding glass door and looked out at her tiny back yard. She had enough names and dates in her head to choke a horse, but for some reason all the facts didn't fit together smoothly. It felt like a jigsaw puzzle where the pieces looked like they should fit, but in reality they were just slightly off, slightly skewed, so there were small spaces between the pieces. What was she missing? And how was she going to find out?

Well, hell, she thought wryly; might as well go to the source.

She sat back down again and checked phone listings. There it was in black and white: Pilar Archuleta, same address. Apparently the woman wasn't concerned with having a public listing, nor of showing herself as a likely single woman, rare for this day and age.

Taking a gulp of air, Lacey dialed the number.

Three rings. Four. At a hundred and one, the woman probably could not move quickly. Would voice mail kick in before she got to the phone? Did she even have voice mail?

Five rings. Six. Seven.

"*Hola?*" The voice was quiet but firm. There was a trace of vibrato to it.

"Mrs. Archuleta? My name is Lacey Fitzpatrick. I'm a private investigator, and the Mission San Juan Capistrano has asked me to investigate"—How to say this?—"spirit activity near the mission. Because you live close by, I was wondering if I could talk to you about it?"

There was silence on the other end, although Lacey could tell the line was still open.

"*Spirito?*" the woman finally asked.

"Yes." Lacey suddenly remembered Father David saying Pilar did not speak English well. How much did she understand? Lacey took Spanish in high school, but rarely used it. She probably remembered just enough to get herself into trouble. She plunged.

"*Spirito... Diablo?*"

She thought she heard an intake of breath. There was silence again for a moment, then a string of Spanish too rapid for Lacey to catch anything familiar.

"Wait," she pleaded. "Stop. *Alto.*" She probed her brain for the old conversational Spanish. "*Lo siento,*" she began slowly. "*Solomente tengo poquito Espaniol. Poquito.*" She hoped that made sense.

"*Poquito?*" the woman asked.

"Yes. *Si.* Speak English?"

"*Poquito,*" she said.

Great, Lacey thought. *I have a tiny bit of Spanish and she has a tiny bit of English. Now what?*

"*Nieto,*" Pilar said. "Mi nieto."

Nieto? Lacey pulled her laptop to her and plugged the word into Google. *Nieto…* granddaughter.

"*Si?*" Lacey asked. "*Nieto* speaks English?"

"*Si. Nieto. Carmen Trujillo. Ocho, quatro, cinco…*"

"Wait," Lacey said. She grabbed her pen and wrote the name. "Okay, *numero?*"

Pilar rattled off the phone number. Lacey just hoped she had the numbers right. She used to get some of them mixed up if she didn't say them in order. She read them back to Pilar.

"*Si,*" the woman said, then another string of Spanish.

"Can I call her?" Lacey asked. "I call—telephone—Carmen?"

"*Si, si,*" Pilar said. More Spanish.

"Okay," Lacey said, feeling heartened by getting this far. "I will call her. Thank you. *Gracias.*"

"*Si,*" Pilar said again. Then she hung up.

Lacey stared at the phone. That was weird, but it certainly seemed like Pilar understood what Lacey wanted. And if she was willing to bring in a translator, she was open to talking about it. Hoping she was reading this right, Lacey dialed the number.

The line rang three times and went to voice mail. A male voice, with a generic message, no name, no number. It looked like Carmen was more careful than her grandmother.

"Hi, this message is for Carmen Trujillo. My name is Lacey Fitzpatrick. I was given your number by your grandmother, Pilar Archuleta. I'm a private investigator and I would like to talk to her about a situation there in her neighborhood. I don't speak a lot of Spanish and it sounds like she doesn't speak much English, but I think what she was saying was that you could act as interpreter for us. Please call me back and let me know if this is something you'd be willing to do. My number is…"

Lacey laid the phone down and wondered how long she'd have to wait for a call back. She'd fully expect Carmen to call Pilar and verify what Lacey said, so it wouldn't be right away. Might as well see what there was for dinner.

She went to the kitchen and prowled the cabinets. Canned soup. Crackers. In the freezer, frozen chicken fried rice. During her brief stint living with Sam, she had definitely been more creative and ambitious with meal planning, but on her own again, it was tougher to get motivated. She opted for the little carton of rice and popped it in the microwave to nuke while she poured a glass of iced tea.

Her phone, still on the table, chimed. She lunged for it. Wouldn't she know the microwave would start beeping at that exact time?

"Hello?" The caller ID said anonymous. More caution.

"Hello, is this Lacey Fitzpatrick?"

"Yes, it is."

"This is Carmen Trujillo. I got your message."

"Great," Lacey said, popping open the microwave door just so it would stop beeping. "Thanks for returning my call. I'm assuming you checked with your grandmother, so I hope I interpreted our, um, conversation correctly."

"You did. Yes, she wants to talk to you. But she's not my grandmother."

"Oh?" Lacey wondered if that Spanish to English dictionary she'd consulted was wonky.

"She's my great-grandmother."

"Oh, okay. Yeah, that makes more sense, with her being a hundred and one years old. It's amazing that she's still living independently."

"She's... tough," Carmen said. "Stubborn, too. Several of us have tried to get her to move in with family and she won't leave."

"Do you know why?" Lacey asked.

Carmen hesitated. "I'll let her tell you. Sometimes I'm not really sure how... clear-headed she is."

At that advanced age, that wouldn't be a surprise. "Okay. When's a good time to get together?"

"I work days, so it'll have to be an evening or a weekend." She paused. "I could do Friday evening. Say five o'clock?"

"That works," Lacey said. She was just as glad Carmen suggested early evening. Lacey wasn't sure she'd want to approach that house after dark. "Do you know what the situation is there that we're investigating?"

Again that hesitation. "I can guess. Bad vibes, right?"

"You could call it that," Lacey agreed, "although it seems to be more serious than that. The mission is very concerned for the safety of their people, especially their school children."

"The mission?" Carmen was clearly surprised.

"Yes. We met with the director this morning. It seems there have been… attacks lately."

"Attacks," Carmen repeated.

"Yes. Unusual attacks. Invisible attacks."

"You said we."

Lacey wondered if the abrupt switch in topics was more evasion or curiosity.

"My partner and I, Sam Firecloud. He's a medium."

"Sam… I read about him, about you two. You helped in that jogger's murder."

"Right."

"Huh. Well, I'm not sure how much you're going to be able to do with Pilar, but I guess you can try."

Lacey was quiet for a minute. "You don't put much stock in the 'bad vibes'?"

Carmen sighed. "Oh, I don't know. It's a weird house. I don't like being there, never have, but it's never been… creepy, at least not to me. Most of my family won't even set foot in it. I don't think it's that bad."

Lacey digested that. "Good to know," she said. "Well, we'll just see what Sam gets from it." She decided not to mention anything about Sam's first impressions. Let the woman see his reactions firsthand. "So we'll see you there, Friday at five."

"Yeah. See you there."

"Thanks, Carmen. Appreciate your help."

~~~

SIX

Friday at ten minutes to five, Lacey and Sam pulled up in front of the little house. Lacey felt some trepidation parking her car right there; she'd already lost one vehicle to their investigations. She didn't want to lose another one.

Sam was out of the car before her, already standing on the sidewalk as she locked up. He sure seemed in a big hurry to face off with a demon, she thought.

When she glanced up at the house, she was slightly shocked to see the door open and little Pilar standing in the opening, waving them in. And little was right. The woman could not have been five foot tall. She wore a thin housedress and glasses, her gray hair pulled back into a knot at the back of her head. She looked like anyone's granny. All she was missing was a plate of cookies.

They approached the house, Sam looking much more relaxed than Lacey felt. He went directly to Pilar and put out his hand to her.

She took his in both of hers, her watery old eyes crinkling at the corners as she grinned at him.

"*Hola*," she said happily. "Samson?"

"Yes," Sam said. "Nice to meet you. This is my partner, Lacey."

Pilar glanced her way, nodded and smiled, but returned her gaze to Sam. Taking his arm, she pulled him toward the door, chattering happily in Spanish.

So now I'm chopped liver? Lacey said to herself. Feeling a bit of pique, she followed the other two into the house.

It was dim inside, especially after Lacey closed the door behind her. The flat-roofed adobe had very small windows which let in a minimum of light. As her eyes adjusted to the dimness, she noted the front room was a combination kitchen and living area, while a doorway led to a bedroom in the back. The walls held a montage of items: paintings, both folk art and religious; bundles of herbs and flowers tied with string and hanging from nails or hooks; and small wooden shelves that supported more dried flowers, colorful animal figurines and tiny metal milagros. In brighter light, Lacey guessed the room would be a riot of color, but the shadows seemed to keep the crazy mix of colors and styles in check. The smell of herbs, both sweet and pungent, permeated the still air.

Pilar motioned for them to sit in mismatched chairs around a plain wooden table, then went to the kitchen to prepare three cups of hot tea. She talked as she puttered, glancing at them occasionally and smiling, totally unconcerned that they had no idea what she was saying.

Lacey shot Sam a questioning look.

"It's okay," he said in a low tone.

What's okay, Lacey wanted to ask. Was he not getting any sensations? Was the demon not in evidence? What—did the thing go out on the town on Friday nights?

Pilar brought the tea cups on a battered wooden tray and passed them around. She handed out spoons and napkins, plus a small china sugar bowl complete with a tarnished silver baby spoon. She took the chair nearest Sam and watched happily as both Sam and Lacey sweetened their tea.

And still she kept up a running commentary in the rapid Spanish. She picked up a bundle of dried herbs from the table and showed them to Sam, apparently naming the various plants, then waved a hand at the paintings on the walls. Lacey examined the paintings, most done in a primitive style, and noted gatherings of people in bright clothing around trees or springs or within rocky canyon walls. The few religious paintings all seemed to show Mary, or at least a Madonna-style woman, crowned with light. Lacey glanced around but saw no evidence of a crucifix or any portrayals of Jesus.

The sound of car tires on gravel drifted through the open windows, and then Lacey heard the thud of a car door closing. Pilar got up and went to open the front door, bringing her great-granddaughter in to join them.

"Hi," Lacey said, sticking out her hand. "I'm Lacey. This is Sam. Sam, this is Carmen Trujillo."

Carmen shook hands and sat at the table, tossing car keys down in front of her. She was almost as short as her great-grandmother, but dark-haired and only in her mid-twenties. Pilar questioned her, motioning to her cup of tea, but Carmen shook her head. The girl was not nearly as pleased to meet them as Pilar had been.

"So, what do you want to know?" she asked abruptly.

Lacey pulled out her digital recorder and glanced at Sam, but he left it to her. She turned back to Carmen.

"Would you ask her if she knows what this spirit is that's emanating from this area?"

Carmen put the question to Pilar. The old woman nodded immediately and spouted a string of Spanish.

"She says he calls himself Reyes," Carmen said.

"Reyes?" Lacey knitted her brows in concentration. "As in *el rey*, the king?"

Carmen confirmed with Pilar. "Yes, that's right."

"Huh." *Not lacking in confidence, is he,* Lacey thought. "What else can she tell us about him?"

The three-sided exchange was maddeningly slow, but eventually produced results.

"She says he is consumed with power, and he gains it by frightening, threatening, even killing people. She says he has killed before."

As Carmen spoke, her eyes slid away from Lacey and she fidgeted at the table. Lacey knew the signs of discomfort.

"Do you believe that?" she asked.

Carmen glanced uneasily at Pilar. "She's said things like this before. Most of us in the family don't… don't take it literally."

Lacey tried to interpret that. "Is she still sharp? Clear-thinking?"

"We think so. At least most of the time. But this…"

"Who has he killed?" Sam asked suddenly. He asked the question of Carmen, but his eyes were on Pilar.

Carmen relayed the question, and Pilar reeled off a response, not to her great-granddaughter but directly to Sam.

"She says he killed her husband and her father. But we know that's not true. They both died of heart attacks."

Lacey made a note to herself in her notebook.

"She says he doesn't like men."

Lacey glanced at Sam. He didn't seem concerned with that pronouncement. If anything, he and Pilar seemed to have developed a bond very quickly. She thought back to when they first arrived.

"When we got here today, Pilar knew Sam's name even before we introduced ourselves. How did she know about him?"

"She heard about him in the news. Some case in LA. She was very excited to see him here."

"Huh." Lacey sat back. How weird was that? The mission hired them, but Pilar was excited to see him? "Does she want us to help her? Does she want us to get rid of Reyes?"

The answer was an enthusiastic yes. Pilar's gray head bobbed up and down with her happy response.

"Yes," Carmen said. "She says she is getting old and cannot contain him like she used to. He grows stronger as she grows weaker."

"Contain him?" Sam repeated. "How does she do that?"

Immediately after hearing the question in Spanish, Pilar rose to her feet and began to point to various things around the room.

"Herbs," Carmen said. "Bitter herbs to frustrate him, like wormwood. Cleansing herbs like basil and rosemary, then sweet herbs to stabilize the area."

Pilar moved to some of the shelves on one wall, fingered the objects there, holding them up.

"Milagros," Carmen said. "You know—miracles?" Lacey nodded. She was familiar with the tiny metal fetishes. "She has amulets, incense. She uses everything in her power, but it is no longer enough."

"Is she a *curandera*?" Lacey asked. "A healer?"

Carmen looked uncomfortable. "She does call herself that. We've asked her not to. The liability, you know. But it's been years since anyone has sought her out. Most are afraid to come here."

Lacey's brain was surging into overdrive. "You said she can no longer contain him. Does she know where he comes from? Why he emanates from this house?"

The response was a string of Spanish, some head bobs and some shakes. Pilar moved toward the door to the bedroom and motioned for them to follow.

"She wants you to go with her," Carmen said. "She will show you."

Glancing quickly at each other, Lacey and Sam stood up to follow. Carmen came behind.

Pilar led them into the bedroom, talking, motioning with her hands. She pointed out more dried flowers, dried herbs, small fabric dolls and tiny metal milagros. Then she moved toward the closed closet door and pointed.

"*Cuidado*," she said to Sam.

Lacey knew that word. She touched his arm. "Be careful," she said.

Sam nodded, both to Lacey and to Pilar. The old woman stood aside, her earlier excitement replaced by a worried frown as she wrung her hands. Sam stepped forward and reached for the doorknob, but didn't touch it. Instead he held his open hand over it, barely inches away, and just stood there.

The room was silent except for an occasional creak from aging timbers.

Sam moved his hand upward, his palm facing the door. He was careful not to touch the paint-chipped wood. He stood quietly, head down, eyes half closed.

Lacey chewed on her lower lip. For the first time, she noted the metal hasp on the door above the knob, a locked padlock hanging there. It was grimy with age. *How could a padlock contain a demon*, she thought.

But then again, it obviously wasn't.

Sam's body spasmed slightly, as if a chill gripped him. He pulled his hand away from the door, rubbing his palm on his jeans.

"Okay," he said. "That's enough." He turned back toward the front room, motioning for Pilar to lead the way. The woman immediately began speaking again, but Lacey noted that she closed one hand on Sam's arm and leaned on him for support.

They retook their seats at the table. Pilar kept her hand on Sam's arm, patting it frequently.

"She says she's tried everything she can think of," Carmen translated. "But nothing banishes him. He always comes back, resurges."

Sam looked around the room, at the folk medicine, the charms and cures. "What about the religious aspect?" he asked. "I see she has pictures of Mary. Has she tried exorcism? Holy water? Maybe getting a blessing?"

Carmen put the questions to her, and the old woman responded effusively, shaking her head the entire time.

"Anything of the church enrages him," Carmen said. "If she brings a crucifix in here, it burns or melts. If she puts a picture of the Christ on the wall, it is dashed down and shattered. Only the old magic has any effect. She has gone back to the old ways, to the magic of the Acjachemen."

"What is that?" Lacey asked.

"The people who were here when the Spanish first arrived. Indios. The Spanish called them *Juaneños* after the mission was built."

Pilar spoke again, motioning around the room.

"She has recently redoubled her efforts to contain him, to keep him at bay for your safety, but she does not know how long it will hold him. She fears she grows weaker every day."

"Why does she stay here?" Lacey asked. "Why doesn't she get away from him?"

The answer was short, and as she spoke, Pilar looked deeply into Sam's eyes.

"She says," Carmen translated, "that if she leaves, he will be free. Free to roam, free to grow more powerful. Free to kill."

Lacey watched the silent communication between Sam and Pilar. The old woman stared sadly into his eyes, and he responded by nodding once, then covering her hand with his.

"We'll help you," he barely whispered. "We'll help you."

Pilar did not seem to need a translation. She smiled briefly and patted Sam's arm. "*Gracias*," she said softly.

For a moment they all sat in silence, frozen in time like a tableau. Then Sam cleared his throat. "All right. We have work to do." He stood up, bringing Pilar to her feet beside him. "Thank you," he said to her. "*Gracias.*"

"*Si, si,*" she said, nodding and smiling. She broke into another spate of rapid Spanish.

"She said she looks forward to your help. She knows you will help," Carmen said. She gathered up her car keys as they all headed for the door.

Lacey pulled out her cards and gave one to Carmen and one to Pilar. "If you have any questions, or think of anything we should know, call me," she said.

Carmen looked the card over, then raised her eyes to Lacey's. "Do you really think you can help? She shouldn't be here alone. I don't believe all this"—she waved back at the house—"but I do want my *abuelita* to be in a safe place. She needs to be where she can be cared for."

"We'll do all we can," Lacey said.

Sam leaned down and brushed a kiss across the old woman's papery-skinned cheek. "*Adios*," he said. "For now."

~~~

SEVEN

Lacey didn't even ask, just drove directly to a diner she'd seen on the way down. She and Sam often debriefed over a meal, and she had so many questions now, she could hardly contain them until she parked the car and they went inside. She fidgeted impatiently while Sam perused the menu, then wondered if the waitress could write their orders any slower. Finally when the woman walked away, Lacey leaned across the table.

"Okay, what's going on? What was all that with Pilar? Is she sensitive? What did you get from that closet? What's this guy's story?"

Sam gazed at her, his black eyes sparkling, his mouth curved in just a hint of a smile. "Which question do you want me to answer first?" he asked sardonically.

Lacey snapped her mouth shut and sat back against the booth seat with a huff. She crossed her arms and glared at her partner.

"Relax," Sam said. He sipped his water. "Is Pilar sensitive? Yes, definitely. And not only to him, but to me, too. I think that's why she glommed onto me right away. She knew I was there to help. Like from Carmen, most of what Pilar gets from people is doubt, or downright disbelief. I doubt she's had a supportive, sympathetic visitor in a long time."

"And yet it sounds like the family doesn't like to go there, doesn't want to spend time there," Lacey said. "They must feel something."

"Probably." He nodded. "But a feeling of discomfort is easy to dismiss after the fact, once they're away from it. And it sounds like they're tired of hearing about it. Did you notice what Carmen said when Pilar said Reyes killed her husband and father?"

"Yes. Total disbelief." Lacey got out her notebook and starred that reminder to check into those deaths. "So they just dismiss her wildest claims as the rantings of an old woman," she said.

"Sure. That's easier than believing a demon lives there." Sam stared out the window for a moment, lost in thought. Lacey watched him. She could almost see the wheels turning in that Navajo brain.

"But there's more than that there," he said finally.

"More than... Reyes?" she asked.

"Yeah. There're other spirits there. I can't tell exactly, but there's a mix of the good and the bad. And some are... imprisoned. Suppressed by Reyes. Like they're not strong enough, powerful enough to push past him." Although he sat very still, Lacey could almost see him reaching with his mind, reaching for more information, more feeling. "Some of that rises up from that closet. Not the closet itself, but from that area. I feel like there's a well there, a deep, dark well where those souls emanate from, and that the house—and the closet—were just built on top of it."

Lacey checked her notes. "But you said this was very old. The property records show the house first bought by Pilar's father in 1918."

"It goes back way before that," he said. "There had to be something there before."

"Something before." Lacey made another note to herself. Looked like she was going to have to do some digging.

"Okay," she said, nodding to herself. "So what does Reyes want? What's he hope to gain by terrorizing people?"

"Power," Sam said simply.

Lacey drummed her fingers on the table. "That seems to be a theme with bad guys," she said. "The witches out on the reservation. Drug dealers in Vegas. What is it with people doing anything and everything to attain power? Why do people do that?"

Sam shrugged. "People crave what they don't have."

Lacey stared into those black, bottomless eyes and thought about that. "So you're saying anyone who craves power does so because they feel powerless."

"Well," he said slowly, "that's a huge simplification, of course. The dynamics of the human psyche are rarely that straightforward, and there are usually lots of variations and lots of layers. But basically… yeah."

Now it was her turn to stare out the window, fitting the pieces together in her mind. "So what you're also saying is… Reyes is human. He's not a demon. He's not supernatural."

Sam nodded. "Correct."

"But how does he do what he does? How does he attack people? If Pilar is right, and he's killed at least two, how does he do that?"

"Old magic," Sam said. "Ancient magic. Remember when Carmen mentioned the early Native Americans the Spanish found here?"

"Yeah, the"—she paged through her notes—"Acjachemen."

"An ancient people who lived close to the earth and who understood how to harness its power."

Something in Sam's voice caught her attention. She glanced up. "Like the Navajo?"

He nodded once. "Like the Navajo."

The waitress brought their food. Lacey pushed aside her notebook to make room for her grilled cheese sandwich and fries. She fiddled with her napkin and the salt shaker until the woman left. When they were alone again, she pointed a fry at Sam.

"So how do we fight him?"

He smiled sardonically. "We fight fire with fire. We have to use the same magic he uses."

Lacey munched a French fry and tapped her notes. "I'm guessing we need to find out where Pilar gets her herbs and charms."

"I agree," he said. "I would bet there's a folk market somewhere around here. Carmen should know. I doubt Pilar drives, so someone has to take her."

Another note for Lacey to follow up on. She definitely had work to do. But another issue was nagging at her, one she wasn't anxious to address, simply because it made her very uneasy. She looked down at her lunch.

"What's the deal with him not liking men?" She glanced up. "Did you feel that?"

"Oh, yeah," he said. His voice was casual, but Lacey detected a more serious tone underneath. She waited. "I don't know what's behind it but it was there. We need to find out who Reyes is—or was. We need to find out his story. Once we know what happened to him, we'll know what motivates him."

She nodded, concentrating her attention on her French fries. For a long moment, she sensed Sam just watching her avoiding his gaze.

"What is it, Lacey?" he asked finally.

She flashed him a quick, false smile. "Remember when we were out on the reservation and you wanted me to leave?"

He locked eyes with her. She knew perfectly well that he remembered. He'd pleaded with her to go back to LA, to leave him to face the witch alone because of the danger.

"Your turn now?" he asked in a low voice.

She sighed unhappily. "Yes."

"You refused to go," he reminded her.

"I know," she said miserably.

They were both quiet, but the conversation continued in the silence. Lacey begged with her eyes; his gently but firmly refused.

She huffed out a breath. "All right," she said testily. "But just… be careful, okay?" She snagged another fry. "I don't want you dying of a heart attack," she grumbled.

He stole one of her fries and saluted her with it, smiling crookedly. "At least not for a while, huh?"

She just shook her head. She couldn't even joke about it.

Sam reached out and touched her hand. She knew he wanted to comfort her, and she tried to wrap herself in it, but it wasn't a strong feeling. Just the thought of losing him…

"Hey," he said. She looked up. "We need to talk about something else."

"We do?" She wondered if she'd forgotten anything, but she was usually pretty thorough in her research.

"You know I don't usually nudge," he said.

"Yeah." She was still at a loss, and could only wonder what the dark depths of his eyes were telling her. He continued to rub his thumb gently across the back of her hand.

"How's your arm?" he asked finally.

"My arm? It's fine." She lifted her right shoulder and rotated the arm, showing him there was not even a twinge from the gunshot wound she'd gotten in Vegas. She'd have two scars, one for the entry point and one for the exit point, but beyond that, there was no residual damage. "I don't even think about it anymore," she said.

He nodded slowly. "Good. I know how much it bothered you those few weeks you moved in with me. I know you hated not being able to do all the things you normally do, and you hated being dependent on me. I'm glad that's not an issue anymore."

Lacey frowned. Where was he going with this? She wasn't sure she liked the sound of it.

"It seems to me," he continued, "that we've been just kind of treading water lately. Staying in the same spot. I'm just wondering if it might be time to start moving forward again."

"Moving—" She swallowed nervously. Ducked her head. "You mean us."

"Yes. Us. I love you, Lacey. I know you love me. Usually when two people love each other, they want to spend most of their time together. Being friends with benefits is fine, but… I just think it's time for more." He regarded her intently, his eyes glittering. "What do you think?"

She stared down at the table miserably. She saw her own hand, his covering it, caressing it. Saw his strong, copper-colored fingers being so gentle, so loving. She dragged in a deep breath.

"I'm scared," she whispered.

His thumb stopped moving, then a heartbeat later, started again.

"Of?" he asked.

She sighed. "I'm afraid it won't work. I'm afraid it'll get all wonky again. What if we try to live together again and it doesn't work?" She lifted her eyes to him, her fear and misery clear in the green depths.

"But the thing that made it wonky is gone," he said, tilting his head at her arm. "Neither of us will be dependent on the other. We'll both be equals, just like we are now, when we're working. We each contribute, and together we do more than either of us could on our own."

She nodded, unconvinced. "But what if we can't?" she asked softly. "I-I don't want it all to go belly up. I don't want to lose what we have. I'd rather keep what we have now than take a chance on losing it all."

He sat very still, barely breathing. She saw the change in his eyes, the disappointment. The same disappointment she'd seen when she'd told him she was going back to her own apartment. The pain in her chest was like a hand squeezing her heart.

"All right," he said. His voice was calm, quiet. "But think about this. You're afraid we'll fail. Okay, I understand that. But by not trying, by not moving ahead, isn't that failing already? Isn't not trying the same as failing?" He pulled his hand away from hers. "We've never backed away from anything we've ever tackled, Lacey. And I don't plan on starting now. Just think about that."

She nodded unhappily, wishing she could feel the confidence that was so evident in his voice, his eyes. "All right," she said softly. "I will."

~~~

EIGHT

Saturday morning, after a mostly sleepless night, Lacey forced herself to put everything aside except the case. Worrying about her and Sam did absolutely no good. When she thought about moving back in with him, she felt her stress level rise, and she immediately retreated from the imaginary confrontation. It was safer to keep everything at arm's length. At least for now.

She set up at her laptop and plunged into her research. She had her notebook and phone to one side, a cup of coffee and an English muffin on the other. Barring an earthquake, she was ready to hunker down.

She'd already decided to start with the most current aspects of the case and work backward. She could be relatively assured of some small successes with the more recent issues than with the older ones.

Manuel Archuleta died October 5, 1958. The death record online was painfully lacking in its information. She'd need more. She pulled up a website to request public records from the Orange County Medical Examiner's files. As she typed in the information to identify the record, she wondered if an autopsy had been performed. Many people were opposed to such action performed on their loved ones.

She hit the submit button and went back to her notes.

Next up: Humberto, Pilar's father. Died April 18, 1949. Again, death records had only the barest information. She switched back to the ME's request for information form and sent that one off, too.

She pulled up property records on the house next. The first recording at that address was Humberto in 1918. How could witchcraft be going on there before there was a house? A vacant lot? She guessed that in 1918, a lot of the town of San Juan Capistrano was vacant. She checked city records: the town didn't incorporate until 1961, but there were census records back to 1880. Three hundred and seventy-six people.

One of those had to be Reyes.

She switched back to the property records for the house and recorded the township and range for the location, then did a search on that.

Bingo. An image of an old land grant came up, but for more than the small property. It was for a hectare.

What the heck was a hectare?

She looked that up. One hectare equaled 2.47 acres. *Decent sized piece of property*, she thought. And the land was granted to... Guillermo Casales.

Pilar's grandfather.

She checked the date of the grant. 1888. But try as she might, she could not find anything to tell her if there was any kind of construction built on the property. Not a house, not a barn, not a chicken coop. Which made sense, actually. There was no town council, no planning and zoning commission, no building inspectors. People laid claim to land and built on it as they wished. There was no one to stop them.

She made a new note to check with the city. They might have copies of older records that weren't digitized.

What else? Feeling frustrated by the lack of success, she drummed her fingers on the table. And noticed her now-cold English muffin. She took a bite—meh. Well, she needed to eat. She choked it down and chased it with lukewarm coffee. She really needed to eat more mindfully, but once she started on an investigative thread, everything else just faded away.

She looked up the Indian tribe, the Acjachemen. Like so many extant peoples "discovered" by Europeans, they were quickly brought into the fold of the Catholic Church, but unlike some, seemed content with their lot. They had their own spirituality and mythology—like all people—which revolved around a creator god/cultural hero named Chinigchinich. Not many details had survived, but religious rituals involved the hallucinogenic properties of the datura plant, and Chinigchinich was apparently a guide and judge, monitoring morality and punishing the lack thereof.

Lacey starred that information in her notes. She wondered if any of the old religion was still practiced today.

Which brought her to the folk market. She googled that in San Juan Capistrano, and came up empty. She tried to frame it several different ways: Mexican farmer's market, herbal market, charm market, magic cures. The only hits she got were for ordinary farmer's markets or New Age shops with crystals and singing bowls. She wondered if places like this deliberately kept a low profile in the cyber world. Referrals for folk magic, charms and witchcraft would be more likely passed by word of mouth, not via Twitter or Facebook.

She checked her watch: nine a.m. Late enough to make some phone calls. She picked up her phone and dialed Carmen.

"Hello?"

"Carmen, hi. It's Lacey Fitzpatrick. How are you doing today?"

"I'm fine," Carmen said, her voice vaguely suspicious.

Lacey ignored the tone. "Great. Hey, I have a question for you. Do you know where Pilar gets her milagros? And her herbs? Is there some kind of farmer's market where that stuff is available?"

Carmen hesitated. "You don't believe all that stuff, do you?"

Lacey did her best to keep her emotions in check. She didn't want to offend the girl, since they might need her help, but the disdainful scoffing of Pilar's predicament rankled.

"It's not my job to believe or not believe," she said carefully. "But it is my job to check every aspect of this mystery so we can solve it." She left it at that. What Carmen did with it was beyond her control.

The girl blew out a breath. "There's a market of sorts on the south side of town. It's not… regulated, as you might guess. It's in an abandoned warehouse."

"Okay. What's the location?"

Carmen gave her directions. "There are no signs, obviously, and the door's in the back. The stuff you're looking for is in the back corner. Look for the chickens."

"Got it," Lacey said. "Thanks. I appreciate that."

Carmen wasn't quite ready to end the call, but she seemed to struggle with what she wanted to say. "Uh, you know, if you two can... resolve this thing, at least in Pilar's mind, so she doesn't feel like she has to stay there... well, that would be a good thing. I'd like to see her in better conditions. Not alone."

Lacey softened. "I understand. Believe me, we'll do everything we can."

"Okay." She paused again. "Thanks."

"Sure thing." Lacey keyed off the call. She knew Carmen wanted the best for her great-grandmother. It was just too bad that didn't include believing in her.

Well, she and Sam did. And now they had a clear path to possible solutions.

With some trepidation, she dialed Sam's number.

"Lacey," he said. He sounded not quite awake.

"You up?" she asked with forced cheerfulness.

"Sort of." He yawned. "What's up?"

"Wanna go shopping for magic charms?"

"Yeah?"
"Yeah. I got the details from Carmen."
"Okay, sure." He yawned again. "When?"
"I'll pick you up in twenty minutes. Can you be ready?"
"Bring coffee."
"You got it."

~~~

As they rolled south on the freeway, each with a grande Starbucks in hand, Lacey brought him up to date on her research. She was much more comfortable immersing herself in the work than in their relationship snarls. "I won't get those death records until probably late in the week," she said. "But what I might do on Monday is go down to the city offices, see if I can scare up some other old property records. If you're sure this haunting goes back before Pilar's house was built, there had to be something else there."

Sam nodded, carefully sipping his coffee. "Yeah, I'm sure," he said.

"Okay. Any idea what we're looking for at this magic market?"

"Mmm, not exactly," he admitted. "Something to plug a hole to hell?"

Lacey glanced over, a grim smile on her face. "How about some of that Gorilla Glue that expands to three times its size?"

"Yeah, not exactly sure where we'd put it," he said. "But we can nose around, see what's out there."

Sam guided Lacey to the warehouse, reading her own directions back to her.

"Abandoned?" she said, remembering Carmen's description. "This thing looks like it should be condemned."

The warehouse was a rickety combination of wood and metal that sat on a lot of bare ground with a few sickly weeds. The original wood siding—gone to gray with the paint all peeled off—had been patched here and there with mismatched sections of metal, some flat, some corrugated and all rusty. There were no windows. A few cars were parked in the front lot and along the street. Lacey parked her red Rav4 next to a yellow-dotted-with-rust-spots 1950s pickup.

"Carmen said the door was around the back," she told Sam as they bailed out of the car. She very mindfully locked it.

They walked around to the back. A single metal door stood slightly ajar. Sam pulled it open and walked in first. Lacey followed.

The place was dim, and they both stopped just inside the door to let their eyes adjust to the low light. Lacey's nostrils were immediately assailed with the pungent smells of greenstuff, herbs, sweat and animal droppings. There was a hum of voices, the squawk of chickens and the bleating of goats.

All human sound stopped suddenly.

Lacey stared around the cavernous building. Stalls lined both sides, haphazard constructions of plywood and junk metal, nailed or screwed or roped together in any way possible. The flat surfaces were covered with boxes and baskets of produce: lettuce, peppers, tomatoes, chilies and carrots. Lacey spied several types of roots displayed, but she couldn't put a name to many of them.

Mixed in among the produce were metal pans and trays, knives up to and including machetes, woven baskets, leather sandals, and boxes of video games. Lacey caught the smell of sizzling meat, and noticed puffs of smoke coming from a makeshift grill halfway down the row.

She also noticed that almost every face in the building was watching them.

"Come on," Sam said in a low voice. He began to browse the displays, moving slowly down the row of stalls. Lacey followed, amazed at the multitude of things that crowded the tables. One stall had bananas, plantains... and boxes of socks. Another had onions, chilies, jalapeño peppers ... and cell phone cases. It was a weird mash-up of a farmer's market and a swap meet.

Little by little, the conversations started again, the noise level picking up slightly as they moved further into the center of the building. Lacey made eye contact with several sellers; some smiled, but most did not.

All righty, then, she thought. She could definitely tell when she wasn't welcome. It occurred to her that she was the only white-skinned person in the building. Having her copper-skinned escort may have been her only saving grace.

"What are we looking for?" he asked.

"In the back corner," she said, nodding in that direction. "She said to look for chickens."

The stall furthest down on the right side had chickens. Dead ones hanging from overhead beams; live ones in cages. There were several cartons of eggs displayed—brown, white and green. Next to them were long narrow baskets of chicken feet. No chickens, just the feet.

Lacey gagged.

"Look," Sam said. He pointed out another basket, this one full of milagros. The small metal charms depicted people, animals, hearts, stars. Lacey dipped a hand in and let the milagros fall between her fingers.

Other baskets held herbs: garlic, basil, rosemary. More she couldn't identify. A tinkling sound drew her eyes upward. Hanging from beams overhead—in between the dead chickens—were small round slabs of dark stone, polished to a high gloss. They clattered against each other in the breeze generated by a large box fan on the floor. For the first time Lacey noticed the many extension cords that snaked all around the stalls, leading to lights, fans, radios playing soft mariachi music.

The entire time she and Sam were looking through the items for sale, a tall Hispanic man stood and stared at them. He was so thin as to be gaunt, his cheeks sunken in on his weathered brown face. He did not speak.

Finally Sam met his eyes directly. He inclined his head slightly in a silent greeting; the man answered in kind, just barely dipping his chin. His eyes never left Sam's; Lacey was not included in the exchange.

"I need help," Sam said quietly.

The man did not respond. His dark eyes glittered at Sam without emotion.

Sam waited. So did the man. "Speak English?" Sam asked finally.

The man's lips pulled back in a sneer. "Yes," he hissed, drawing out the word. "I don't sell to cops."

"Not cops," Sam said. He held up his hands in a peace-making gesture. "I need help. Protection. Charms."

The man stood motionless, not making any sign that he might have heard. The two of them stared at each other silently.

Jesus, Lacey thought. *Can we get past the stare-down and get to business?* But she didn't speak.

Finally the man relented. He unclasped his hands from behind his back and motioned toward the milagros.

"Charms," he said.

Sam shook his head. "No. Stronger."

More staring. No blinking. Lacey wanted to shift her feet, relax her stance a little, but didn't dare move.

The man reached over and took one of the small polished slabs down. A hole was drilled in the top of the round, and fishing line was used to hang it. He handed it to Sam.

Lacey craned to see without moving closer to Sam. The slice of stone was dark gray, but so shiny she could clearly see Sam's reflection in it.

"What is it?" she asked softly.

The man's eyes switched from Sam to her, just briefly, as if she were a harmless bug, then returned to Sam.

"Obsidian," he said.

Sam examined the stone mirror closely, then handed it back. "Stronger."

The man's mouth thinned into an angry line. His eyes darted back and forth. Lacey guessed there was some heavy thinking going on.

He reached down underneath the table and pulled out a thin, flat object of the same dark gray obsidian. He handed it to Sam, who held it flat in the palm of his hand so Lacey could see.

A knife. The flaked business edge so sharp, it looked only paper thin. Sam tested the edge carefully with his thumb; it wouldn't take much pressure to slice through the skin. The thing looked delicate, yet Lacey could imagine the quick, effortless bloodletting it could do.

Sam pushed the knife back at the man. "Stronger."

The man huffed out a frustrated breath. He leaned both hands on the table and angled his head down toward the metal cages stacked beside the table.

Lacey glanced down and let out a small squeak when she saw the chickens crowded in the cages. Red hens, black roosters with shiny, arched tail feathers. *What the hell*, she thought. *Sacrifice a live chicken?*

Sam stared at the chickens. *He wasn't really considering that, was he?*

He returned his gaze to the man. "That's all you got?" he asked quietly.

The man crossed his arms over his chest and glared at Sam. Lacey thought he did a pretty good impression of a brick wall.

Sam was still holding the knife, the man having ignored his attempt to give it back. Now he laid it on the table.

"*Gracias*," he said. He turned to go, catching Lacey's elbow and turning her with him toward the door.

Questions flooded her mind, but she held her tongue until they'd walked casually past the stalls and exited the building. Once they'd walked back to the car and climbed in, she released the breath she'd been holding.

"Jesus," she muttered, "what the hell was that? Some kind of pissing contest?"

Sam laughed once without humor. "Yeah, sort of," he said. "He was trying to find out how gullible I was. How much I knew—or didn't know—about magic. About witchcraft."

Lacey started the car. "Well, how much do you know? Was he being straight with you?"

"Pretty much. Not at first, though. He was trying to palm off the usual stuff first, stuff people readily recognize but that doesn't have much power. By the time he got to the obsidian knife, he knew I was a player."

"And what about that?" Lacey asked as she wheeled the car out onto the street. "Was he suggesting we sacrifice a chicken?"

"Yeah. Blood is powerful. Fresh blood, pumping from a still-beating heart, is best. You make a deal with the gods, you gotta offer something serious."

Lacey glanced at him. "But we're not doing that, right?" she asked.

He chuckled, then took her hand and threaded his fingers through hers. "No, we're not doing that. At least, not until we've tried a few other options first."

She glared at him.

"Hey," he said, "I need to pick the kids up at noon. How about we do that, then go grab us some burgers for lunch?"

Lacey wasn't sure if he was trying to throw her off the track with his offer or if he was just being sweet. Probably both. And it was working. She hadn't seen his kids in a couple weeks. The idea of shrugging off the morning's adventure and losing herself in burgers and school news was definitely appealing.

"You're on," she told him. After a second, she added, "Burgers only. No chicken sandwiches."

He just laughed.

~~~

The kids were excited to see Lacey and ride in the Rav4. The little SUV apparently had a much higher "cool factor" than Sam's old truck.

"Guess what I'm going to be for Halloween," nine-year-old Kenzie said from the back seat.

"Seat belts?" Lacey queried. She wouldn't move the car until she heard two clicks, and the kids knew it.

"A seat belt," Daniel guffawed. Lacey saw him poke his sister's side. "You have to be long, flat and gray," he told her.

"No, not a seat belt," Kenzie groaned.

Lacey heard the clicks and pulled out of the parking lot. "I don't know," she said to Kenzie. "A princess? An alien?"

"A witch!" Kenzie said with a wicked grin.

Lacey and Sam traded looks.

"Oh, cool," Lacey said with forced enthusiasm. "You got your costume already?"

"Yeah. It's all black, and Mom's going to paint my face green. I'm gonna be scary."

In the rearview mirror, Lacey saw Kenzie sit up tall and stretch her hands out in claws. A shiver went up her spine.

"What about you, Daniel?" she asked.

"Eh, I don't know if I'm going out," the thirteen-year-old said. His voice was a combination of arrogant disdain and a hint of wistfulness.

"Kid stuff, huh?" Lacey guessed. She caught Kenzie's eyes in the mirror and winked. "You'll miss out on all the candy, though."

"And you're not getting any of mine," Kenzie announced.

Daniel shrugged. "I don't know."

"Well, you've still got a couple weeks to think about it," Lacey said. "So where are we going for lunch?"

Lacey was always amazed at how readily the kids fell back into the comfortable pattern of the four of them as a family. The end of Sam and Lacey's short-lived experiment living together had dismayed them for a time, but now they seemed perfectly okay with the on-again, off-again relationship, as Lacey had been before Sam suggested moving forward. *Thank God kids are so resilient*, Lacey thought. They bounced back quickly from anything that was thrown at them. Quicker than she did. For their sake, she shoved the issue onto a back burner in her mind.

Back at Sam's apartment, burgers in hand, the four made a picnic lunch around the coffee table.

"You know what we should do tonight?" Kenzie said.

"What?" Sam asked.

"We should make a blanket fort and turn off all the lights and tell ghost stories. That would be fun."

Sam, next to Lacey on the couch, arched an eyebrow at her. "Sounds good to me," he said softly. "Wanna share my blanket fort tonight?"

Lacey's breath caught in her throat, but when she looked into his dark eyes, she realized he was not pushing. If anything, he was offering an olive branch. His eyes sparkled and his mouth looked soft and inviting. He had that look that made her toes curl. "I could do that," she said with a smile. She stretched up to kiss him and seal the deal.

"Yea!" Kenzie said, clapping.

Daniel looked away in embarrassment. "Yuck!"

Sam and Lacey both laughed.

~~~

NINE

Monday morning Lacey took her time making sure she had all her notes and research regarding Pilar's property before she left for San Juan Capistrano again. She'd printed out a copy of the 1888 land grant, as well as all the more current property records. She knew she'd get further with the Planning and Zoning Department if they could see she'd done her homework.

She arrived at the city office a little after ten; past the early morning crush, but before the pre-lunch slowdown. She made her case to an administrative assistant named Dorothy Simpson.

"I'm a private investigator doing some research into this property here," she said, passing the land grant across the counter. "What records might you have about anything built on that property?"

Dorothy, a slender black woman with kind eyes, listened patiently. "Hmm," she said, checking the legal description. "We've got some old plat books from 1901. Hang on just a moment and let me see what I can find."

Feeling hopeful, Lacey parked on a chair in the waiting area and looked around. The city building was clearly modern with linoleum floors and dropped ceilings. She wondered if they had a back archive full of dusty old books. The mission, after all, was founded in 1776. Lots of history hereabouts.

Dorothy had only been gone about fifteen minutes when Lacey heard her heels tapping the floor on her return. She jumped to her feet and met the woman back at the counter.

"Here we go," Dorothy said as she laid the heavy book on the counter. The book was leather-clad and oversized, its pages somewhere between legal-sized and tabloid. Dorothy opened the cover carefully and paged through. Lacey, much as she would have liked to take charge, let Dorothy scan the range and township numbers at the corners of the pages.

Those pages, Lacey could see, were heavy paper, and the plat diagrams were all hand-drawn, of course.

"Do you have a lot of older stuff like this that's not digitized?" she asked.

"Oh, yeah," Dorothy said. "We have an intern that was working on that over the summer, but of course she's back in school now. I'm afraid it's a low priority, and very time-consuming."

Lacey could imagine. What Dorothy didn't say, but Lacey guessed, was that the budget for preserving such archives was very low, as well. Most city officials were more concerned with the future than the past.

"Ah," Dorothy said suddenly. She smoothed the page and double-checked the number against her note, then turned the book around on the counter so Lacey could see it right side up.

"This is El Camino Real Street," she said, pointing out the narrow road. "Here's the mission on this side, and your property is here, across the street."

Lacey stared down at the faint drawing and tried to reconcile it in her mind with the current Google map she'd printed out.

"Is this... a building?" she asked, pointing to a square set back from the road.

Dorothy looked closer. "Yes. See the double lines around the outside? That designates a building, probably a house. Back here," and Dorothy tapped another, smaller square behind, "is probably a stable or a barn. No double lines on that one."

Lacey looked closer. So Guillermo had a house. Where was it compared to Pilar's?

She pulled the Google map out of her notebook and spread it next to the plat map. She lined up the road on both maps. The scale was wrong; the Google map had smaller dimensions, but she thought she could make a decent comparison.

The house was roughly in the same spot.

"This is current?" Dorothy asked, tapping the Google map.

"Yes." Lacey frowned down at the two documents.

"Then it's the same place," Dorothy said. She smiled at Lacey.

"But there's a discrepancy," Lacey said. She pulled out the property records. "The first modern record of sale of the property is 1918, and later records show the house built in that same year. If the house was already there, wouldn't the records show an earlier year?" She passed the document to Dorothy.

"Hmm, yes, you're right. It should. That's odd." Dorothy tapped her chin as she pondered that. "All right. Let me go check something else." She pulled the book back, ready to close it up.

"Uh, can I possibly get a scan of this?" Lacey asked.

Dorothy nodded. "Sure. You'll need to fill out this request form. It takes five business days, but put your email address down and we'll send it to you."

Before passing the form to Lacey, Dorothy jotted the book number and page number in the appropriate place.

"Great," Lacey said, taking the paper. "I'll fill the rest in while you're looking for the next thing."

Dorothy was only gone ten minutes that time. She returned with another book, canvas-covered, and legal-sized. She flipped through this sturdier book with more speed.

"This is from 1915," she said. She found the page with the correct coordinates and showed Lacey. "Here's the house." Again, the double outline of the structure showed up.

"Well, something's wrong," Lacey said. "Was there any kind of change in how records were recorded around 1918? Some transfer or conversion of records that would have marked the house newly built in 1918 when that wasn't so?"

Dorothy frowned. "Not that I'm aware of, and I've been here for almost twenty years." She scanned the drawing more closely, checking all the fine print around the legend and the edges. Finally she flipped the page over and looked at the back.

"Oh," she said with dawning understanding. "Look at this. Here's a note that was added later." Again she turned the book so Lacey could see.

House and shed both burned completely down to the ground. –March 5, 1917.

"Okay," Lacey said. "This makes sense, then. The house was destroyed, then they built a new one the next year."

"Yes," Dorothy said. "I knew there had to be an answer." She smiled, pleased they had solved the riddle.

"Can I get a copy of this drawing, as well?" Lacey asked. "Front and back?"

"Sure." Dorothy handed her another request form.

By the time Lacey left the office, she felt like she had a good handle on the history of the house. The first home was built somewhere between 1888 and 1901. That definitely qualified as old. She realized this didn't really offer much insight into who Reyes was or when he began haunting the property, but at least she knew there was something there to haunt.

That evening she called Sam and told him what she'd found.

"Okay, I think that kinda makes sense," he said. "When we were there and I was feeling the space around that closet, it felt… mismatched, like it didn't line up somehow. I'm still not sure what that means, but remember I said it was like the house—and the closet—were built over something that was already there?"

"Yes," Lacey said. "So Reyes comes from before. Whatever happened to set him in motion happened before." She had a thought. "Do you think Pilar's father might have built the new house to... contain him? Try to keep him buried?" She had an image in her head of the Wicked Witch of the West's feet sticking out from under the fallen house in *The Wizard of Oz*.

"Hmm, possible," Sam said. "I'm not sure why you'd want to rebuild a house on already haunted ground, but if you did, you probably would try to cover the area over. It didn't work, obviously." He paused for a moment, and Lacey knew he was thinking hard. "I need to walk the property again," he said. "Can you set it up with Carmen?"

"Sure," she said. "When?"

"How about Wednesday? I'll take the day off from work."

"Okay by me, but remember, Carmen works days, too," Lacey said. "I doubt she'll be thrilled about having to take time off to translate for us."

"Oh, yeah," he said, disappointed. "But you know what? She doesn't need to be there. We got a lot of information from Pilar last time, so I don't think we'll need an interpreter this time. But can you have her notify Pilar, so she knows we're coming?"

"You got it," Lacey said. "If need be, I might be able to tease out a little bit from Pilar, but we'll just see how it goes."

"With any luck, I'll get everything I need from my walk. If I don't, we'll get with Carmen another time."

"Okay, boss." Lacey grinned. "I'll set it up." She could feel the excitement building.

They were on the hunt now.

~~~

TEN

Wednesday morning, Lacey pulled up the dirt driveway in front of Pilar's house and parked the car. She still wasn't totally comfortable with leaving her car in Reyes' sphere of influence, but Carmen had parked there without incident, so…

Pilar came out the front door to greet them.

"*Hola. Buenos dias,*" she called cheerfully.

"*Buenos dias,*" Lacey said. "*Como esta usted?*"

"*Bien, bien,*" Pilar said. She linked one arm with Sam for the walk into the house, but then pulled Lacey closer and linked arms with her as well.

Hey, Lacey thought, *maybe I'm not chopped liver anymore.*

Pilar chattered happily as they went inside.

The house looked much the same. Lacey noticed the smell of herbs seemed stronger, more pungent. She noted some fresh bundles replacing some of the dryer ones she'd seen last time. She fingered one that rested on the table.

"New herbs," she said quietly to Sam.

He nodded. "Keeping him at bay."

Pilar immediately began assembling items for tea: cups, spoons, sugar.

"Can you tell her to wait?" Sam asked Lacey. "I want to walk first."

Lacey tapped Pilar on the shoulder. When the old woman turned, Lacey laid her hands over the tea cups. "Later," she said, racking her brain for the right words. "*Otro hora, por favor.*"

Pilar got it. She nodded and smiled.

"Sam," Lacey said, pointing to him, "walk." She made a walking pantomime with her fingers.

"*Si,*" Pilar said. She responded in a spate of Spanish, motioning toward the bedroom.

"Yes," Sam said. "I walk there." He pointed to himself, made the walking fingers and pointed toward the door.

Pilar nodded and led the way. The three of them trooped into the bedroom, then Pilar stood aside to give Sam room. He approached the closet carefully. The padlock was still in the hasp, but unlocked. He pulled it out and handed it to Pilar.

Lacey held up her phone and started filming.

She noticed that he wasn't quite as hesitant as he had been before. He approached the closed door and actually got closer than last time. He held his hands out flat, inches from the door, and tuned in to the sensations.

Lacey began worrying her bottom lip in her teeth. She glanced over at Pilar. The woman held herself tensely, but didn't seem overly worried.

Suddenly Sam reached for the door knob.

Lacey gasped.

He curled his hand around the knob, gingerly at first, then more confidently. He turned the knob slowly.

The door swung open.

Lacey angled her phone toward the opening and stared at the screen. Clothes hanging in the dim recess, shoes on the floor. No movement.

Sam stepped into the open doorway.

Lacey could hardly keep still. Sounds seem to crawl up her throat and demand to be uttered, sounds of caution, of dread, but she clamped her jaws tight to keep them contained. Her eyes darted to Pilar; again, the woman looked watchful, concerned, but not panicky.

Then Sam was closing the door again. The click of the lock mechanism was a welcome sound. Lacey let out a long, slow breath.

"We need to go outside," he said. He caught Pilar's gaze and pointed toward the front. "Outside," he said again.

Pilar nodded, but motioned for Sam to go first. He moved past Lacey, giving her a quick smile. "Come on."

They trooped out the front door. Sam turned left and walked around the side of the house. The small window on the outside wall showed where the living room was, and beyond that, a solid wall backing the closet and bedroom.

Sam walked close to the wall, his soft knee-high moccasins making no mark on the hard earth. He held one hand out to the wall, not touching it, but letting it glide along just inches from the rough adobe surface. As he neared the midsection of the wall, he slowed.

Lacey watched through her screen as she filmed. He eased to a stop, then stepped out away from the wall. He walked a small semi-circle, around and back, his eyes intent on the ground. *Was he looking for something?* Lacey couldn't be sure. With Sam, she never knew if he was looking with his eyes or with his inner senses.

Suddenly he stopped and crouched on the ground. With one hand, he scratched at the dirt. The dry ground resisted most of his attempt to dig into it, so he stood and pulled a quarter from his pocket. He tried again, and was able to gouge out a hole a couple inches deep and a few inches wide.

Lacey glanced at Pilar. The woman seemed as lost for an explanation as Lacey was. *What was he looking for?*

He scratched at the hole, enlarging it slightly, digging deeper. Most of his hand disappeared into it. Then he stopped, examined the hole and began to dig in earnest.

"Pilar," he called, "do you have a shovel?" He made a digging motion.

Pilar mimicked his pantomime. "*Si*," she said. She turned and disappeared back into the house, then returned with a garden trowel.

Sam frowned at the lightweight tool, but took it. He stabbed the ground with it, knocking loose chunks of hard dirt, then scraped them away. The hole widened, deepened.

Then the trowel was stopped suddenly with a dull *thunk*.

Sam cleared more dirt away. Lacey edged closer, video recording, until she could film over his shoulder. She saw the striations of wood grain, the rough wood the same color as the earth around it.

"What is that?" she asked.

Sam looked up at her. "I think," he said slowly, "it's stairs."

~~~

ELEVEN

"Stairs?" Lacey couldn't keep the surprise out of her voice.

"Yeah," Sam said grimly. "I think there's a cellar or basement or something here." He dug a little more with the trowel, then picked up a piece of something gray.

"What's that?" Lacey asked.

Sam held it up in his hand and turned it in the sun. It glittered with a dull gleam. "Obsidian," he said.

Pilar's voice, soft with respect, drifted to them. "*Brujo*," she said.

Sam nodded. "Yes. Witch."

Lacey felt light fingers brush her spine. The chill that went through her shook the camera. She stepped back and planted her feet squarely on the ground to give her more stability.

Sam rose to his feet and whacked dirt from his knees. "We have to dig here," he told Lacey. "We'll have to come back with shovels and dig. Remember I said there was a deep well here? That the evil was coming from there?"

"Yeah."

"This is it. This is where it comes from."

Lacey didn't like this, not one little bit. They were going to dig *down* to the evil?

"But you don't really mean *we* have to do this?" she asked. "You and me? I mean, can't we get someone to do that? Call in a contractor, someone with a backhoe?" The idea of the two of them digging, without any more protection than the clothes they wore, gave Lacey the willies.

Sam was shaking his head. "No. We can't dig like that. It has to be by hand." He locked eyes with her. "This is the key, Lacey. We have to do it. We have to get down there."

She turned off her phone and shoved it in her pocket. "Okay," she said reluctantly, "if you say so. Do you want to go get some shovels and start today?"

He stared down at the ground, then took Lacey's wrist and checked her watch. "No. I'd rather start early in the morning. Saturday. I'll see if Ed can help us." He paused, thinking. "Once we start, we have to keep going and get down there. We can't stop." He looked up at Lacey. "Reyes is not going to like this."

Lacey swallowed. "Yeah, I'll bet he won't," she said unhappily.

Using his feet, Sam scraped the loose dirt back into the hole. He handed the trowel back to Pilar.

"Can you make her understand?" he asked Lacey.

"Uh, I'm not sure," she said. She racked her brain for the word dig. It wasn't there. "*Sabado*," she said to Pilar. She pointed to herself and Sam. "*Sabado*, we come back, dig *aqui*." She pantomimed as she spoke.

"*Sabado?*" Saturday?

"*Si*," Lacey said. "Okay? We dig." She pointed to the hole.

Pilar wrung her hands nervously. "*Si*." She smiled briefly, but it was not convincing.

Sam stepped up to the woman and put his hands on her frail shoulders. "We're going to fix this," he said earnestly. "We're going to get rid of Reyes."

Lacey doubted Pilar understood the words—except for *Reyes*—but she seemed to understand the intent. She nodded. "*Si*," she said quietly.

"Come on." Sam put his arm around her and led her back to the house.

~~~

Melissa Bowersock

TWELVE

Friday morning, Lacey had some welcome emails waiting for her. She was grateful for something to take her mind off the plans for tomorrow, even if it was all related.

Sam had called Ed LaRosa, his ex-wife's husband, and convinced him to help with the digging project. As a bonus, Ed spoke Spanish, so he was able to call Pilar and explain the plan more eloquently than Lacey could. Both Lacey and Sam preferred this to going through Carmen. They weren't sure how supportive the girl would be, or if she might even try to stop them. Dealing directly with Pilar—as directly as possible—gave them all some needed confidence.

So when Lacey sat down to her laptop and saw the two emails from the San Juan Capistrano Planning and Zoning Department, she was glad for the slight diversion. She printed out the scans of the old plat drawings and tried again to line them up with the current Google map. It was a struggle to get the scale right; she printed out several attempts before she got the Google map to line up exactly with the old maps using the street as a registration mark. When she finally got the streets to match up perfectly, she then checked the two versions of the houses on the property.

Pilar's house was not built in the same footprint as the older house. To Lacey's eyes, judging by the scale of the maps, the houses overlapped, but Guillermo's had been situated several feet further south.

Directly over the stairs that Sam found.

She sat back in her chair and stared out the slider. So it could have been a cellar. The fact that Sam was correct did not instill comfort.

What was down there?

She decided to switch away from the disturbing thoughts to something else. She had two emails from the city's office of the medical examiner: Humberto's and Manuel's death records.

She opened Humberto's first. She would expect, his death being so much earlier, that there would be less detail.

She was right.

April 18, 1949, Humberto Maria Casales died of an aortic aneurysm. No prior damage to the heart muscle, no thickening of the arteries. Hmm, Lacey thought. That's not a heart attack. An aneurysm was a weak spot in an artery wall that bursts suddenly. Normally drops a victim in an instant and they're dead before they hit the ground. Attached to the file was a brief sketch of the rupture in the aorta above the heart.

No mention by the attending physician of any prior treatment for heart-related issues. And back in 1949, she wasn't sure if anyone had even heard the word cholesterol.

She opened the file for Manuel. He died October 5, 1958.

Severely ruptured thoracic aortal aneurysm.

That word *severely* gave her pause. She was no doctor, but she would consider any ruptured aneurysm to be pretty damn severe. Funny, though, that both men died of the same cause.

She scanned the ME's description. Some prior scarring of the heart muscle. Manuel was being treated for high blood pressure. *Must have had a small incident earlier*, Lacey guessed. What were those mini-strokes called? TIAs, she thought. So at least here was some physical evidence to support the idea of a heart attack.

She read further. More physical details about his other organs, all normal. He'd been overweight, but not obese. There was some slight bruising on the skin of his upper chest. Then one sentence leaped out at her.

Rupture was so forceful that aorta was completely severed.

Severed? She read the sentence again. Severed, as in torn in half, completely pulled apart. Could an aneurysm do that?

She looked at the diagram included at the back of the file. The rupture was in the aortal arch. Lacey knew the aorta—the main artery that carried blood from the heart—left the top of the heart and then arched over it 180 degrees before heading down behind the heart to supply the lower half of the body. The diagram showed the break—the rupture—as a dashed line clear across the top of the arch.

She clicked back to the file on Humberto and brought up that older, cruder diagram. She sized the windows on her computer so she could look at both diagrams side by side.

The rupture was the same. Both diagrams showed the aorta had been ripped completely in half.

Jesus Christ, she thought.

Her body turned cold.

~~~

She wasn't sure how long she stared at the screen, mindless, her eyes glazed over and unseeing. Her phone chimed at her, but she just shoved it aside. That broke the spell, though. She stood up and paced the room.

This was… insane. No one could do this. Could they? How could a ghost, a spirit, reach into a living human's body and *rip their aorta apart*?

She pushed the idea aside angrily and went to the kitchen. Chugged OJ right from the bottle.

No. It was impossible.

She put the juice back in the fridge and shoved the door closed.

She had to stop this, get away. Put her brain on hold for a while. She strode into her bedroom and changed quickly into sweats, then grabbed her keys and left the apartment. The exercise room was just down at the end of the building. She hadn't worked out in a while. A hard, focused workout would do her good.

She warmed up gradually on the treadmill, then did sit-ups, pull-ups, push-ups. On a Friday morning the place was deserted, so she had no qualms about throwing herself into the exercises with fierce intensity, grunting loudly as she pushed herself beyond her usual limits. Sweat streamed down the sides of her face as she did lat pulls and crunches on the weight machine. She kept at it until her muscles began to scream in protest, bunching and cramping in her calves and thighs. Only when a cramp lanced up into her hip and paralyzed her entire leg did she drop to a mat on the floor and suck in deep drafts of air through her mouth.

Her heart hammered in her chest.

She thought again of those severed aortas.

Jesus Christ.

Back in her apartment, she peeled off the wet sweats and took a long shower. The stinging pulses of water massaged her aching muscles and felt heavenly.

Heavenly?

She twisted off the water, dried and dressed. Still combing her wet hair, she went to the kitchen and scanned the cupboard for lunch ideas.

Soup. What was it about cool, crisp fall air that made soup sound good? She pulled out a can of chicken noodle. Like her mother used to fix when she was sick as a child.

Yeah, she was sick, all right. Sick at heart.

She forced herself to make a proper lunch setting at the table, not just eat standing up. She brought her bowl, set it on a placemat with spoon and napkin, flanked by a glass of iced tea. Anything to focus on, anything to keep her mind from gravitating back to the morning's revelations.

But once she sat down to eat, her mind took over.

There was something here, though, something beyond the grisly images in her brain. She remembered hearing a long time ago about something called psychic surgery. When she was still with the LAPD, there'd been something about this weird practice being performed by Philippine immigrants—people with no formal medical training at all treating their poor countrymen.

She pulled her laptop close and started a search.

Yup; there it was. Psychic surgery. People who professed to be able to remove evil spirits, noxious tumors, even diseased organs without ever breaking the skin. There were even YouTube videos of some of the processes. Lacey noticed that the camera angles were usually very bad, often blocked by the "surgeon's" activities, so very little contact was visible. The practitioners performed some sort of quick massage of the skin with their bare fingers, then miraculously produced blobs of dark, ugly tissue that they claimed was causing the illness. There was never an incision, never any blood. The patients were awake and aware, and of course reported feeling better instantly.

So was this what Reyes was doing, albeit in a much less helpful way? Lacey noticed that some psychic surgeons professed to be guided by God, others by more obscure entities or powers, but all seemed to accord their ability to supernatural forces. White magic.

But white magic could be turned to black.

Lacey finished her soup and checked the time. Twelve-thirty. She wondered if she might be able to catch Sam on his lunch break. Working construction, he didn't necessarily stop to eat at the same time every day. She took a chance and called him.

"Hey," he said upon answering.

"Hey," she replied. "Are you on lunch? Got some info for us."

"I am," he said. "What did you find?"

She swallowed. "It's not good."

First she told him about the juxtaposition of Pilar's house to her grandfather's.

"The old house absolutely sat over that place where you found the stairs. It's very possible that after the first house burned down, the stairs got filled in with dirt and rubble. Maybe Pilar's father wasn't even aware of them when he built the second house."

"Possible," Sam said thoughtfully. "Although I did get a sense that the second house was built as an attempt to... block the energy. Keep it contained. Like putting a lid on an oil well."

Lacey snorted. "Well, that didn't work, did it?"

"So what else?" Sam pressed.

"It gets worse," she said. "I received the detailed death records of both Pilar's father and husband. Both died the same way. Something reached inside their chests and ripped their aortas in half."

Sam let out a low whistle. "Holy shit."

"Exactly," Lacey said.

"But, reached inside..." he started.

"There were no wounds on the outside of the bodies. No incisions. Oh, Manuel's records mention some bruising on the chest, but that's all. No entry wounds." She paused. "Have you ever heard of psychic surgery?"

"Yes, I have," he said. "You think it's something like that?"

"That's the only thing I know of that sounds comparable. You know how it is; some people swear absolutely it's true, but there's no empirical proof. It's never been studied by modern medicine."

"Right," Sam said. "It's considered folk medicine or outright chicanery."

"And I don't care what people call this," Lacey said, "I think it's real. There's no other explanation for it. People's aortas don't just rip apart."

He was quiet for a moment. "No. I would think not."

She let him absorb that for a bit, then addressed her real worry. "Sam, I—I don't want you to go digging there tomorrow. I mean, Pilar said Reyes hates men. What if he—"

"Lacey." He stopped her, his voice firm but gentle. "We've been over this ground before. We can't let the bad guys win. We can't walk away. You know that."

"So get someone else to go dig it up," she pleaded.

"Oh, just send someone else in to get *their* aortas ripped in half? Come on, Lacey. Be smart. We can't send someone else in to get killed."

Panic rose up in her chest. "But I don't want *you* to get killed." She could feel tears behind her eyes, hear them in her voice.

"Lacey." He breathed her name, half comforting, half admonition. "I have no intention of getting killed. I know what we're up against. I'll take every precaution. If I feel I'm in any danger—"

"What precautions?" she demanded. "How can you guard against this? Wear a bullet-proof vest? A suit of armor?"

She heard him blow out a long breath. "All right. Listen to me, Lacey. If you don't want to go tomorrow, that's okay. Ed and I can do this. He can talk to Pilar. If you want to sit this one out, I totally understand."

Sit it out? Sam could very literally be walking into his death, and he said she could *sit it out?* Not be there? Not watch? As if she could sit at home alone, waiting for a phone call?

"Are you crazy? I can't—"

"Lacey." He sighed. "I love you. You're my partner. I'm not going to do anything to mess us up. I mean it." His voice dropped to a low tone. "Trust me on this?"

"Uh—" She knew arguing was useless. She could never talk him out of this. She struggled to get her panic under control, to contain the feeling of dread that filled her. To feel instead the love and the confidence that was in his voice. She did trust him, to the ends of the earth and back.

But she didn't trust Reyes.

"All right," she barely whispered. "But you said every precaution. I'll hold you to that. I want every defense you can think of, I don't care if it's witchcraft or voodoo or whatever the hell. We'll sacrifice a chicken if we have to. We'll—"

He chuckled into the phone. "That won't be necessary. But I'll tell you what. I'll pick you up a little early. We'll go get some extra safeguards before we meet Ed at Pilar's."

"Safeguards?"

"Yeah. You'll see."

Lacey still felt edgy, but Sam's quiet confidence was soothing. So was hearing him say he loved her.

"Okay," she agreed in a small voice.

"Great. Hey, I need to get back to work. I'll see you first thing in the morning, okay?"

"Yeah." She paused and licked her lips. "Sam?"

"Yeah."

"I love you."

"I love you, too, Lacey. Don't worry. We're going to be fine."

She could only pray that was true.

~~~

THIRTEEN

Lacey was ready when Sam pulled up outside her apartment in his battered blue truck. Instead of his soft moccasins, he wore his work boots; otherwise his uniform was the same as always: jeans and a t-shirt. His long hair, pulled back in a ponytail, gleamed blue-black in the sun.

Lacey came out to meet him and glanced into the bed of the truck. "Got enough tools?" she asked.

There were two round-point shovels and one square-point, plus a couple of heavy duty spades and a pickaxe. There was also a hard plastic cooler full of bottled water and ice.

"I think so," he said. She climbed into the cab beside him and he immediately pulled her into his arms. She settled gratefully against his chest, taking in the clean smell of his lean, muscular body.

He squeezed her once for good measure and tipped her face up to his, brushing a kiss across her mouth.

"Come on," he said. "Let's go."

She nodded and pulled back so he could drive the truck, but she rested her hand on his thigh.

She was surprised when he passed the offramp for Pilar's. He continued south another couple of miles, then exited the freeway in the dodgy end of town. She glanced over and angled a questioning look at him.

"Safeguards, remember?" he said.

He pulled into the lot in front of the warehouse. Even this early, there were cars there.

They strode inside with the confidence of knowing where they were going. Sam made a direct line to the chicken man down at the end of the row of stalls.

The man looked up in surprise. He remembered them—*how could anyone not recognize Sam*, Lacey thought. But as before, he said nothing, just waited and watched.

Sam perused the table. He bypassed the milagros, but picked up several tied bunches of herbs and set them in the center of the table. He pointed to the obsidian mirrors. "Give me four of those," he said.

The man's eyebrows arched up, but he immediately pulled four stone slices off the display and laid them down next to the herbs.

"One obsidian knife," Sam said.

The man produced an open cardboard box of knives. Sam pored through, checking the edges. Finally he chose one, set it with the other things and nodded.

"How much?"

The man put away the box and calculated in his head.

"One hundred," he said.

Lacey gasped. "A hundred? For some herbs and pieces of stone? Sam—"

"One hundred," Sam said. He was already peeling off twenties from a wad of bills. He counted them off and handed them to the man. The vender checked them again and slid the bills into his own pocket.

"Want a bag?"

"Sure," Sam said.

The man scooped up the items and laid them carefully in a plain brown sack.

"Thanks," Sam said as the man handed him the bag. He turned to go.

Lacey saw the hint of a smile on the man's face.

"Sam," she hissed as they walked out. "That was way too much for that stuff. Did you see how many of those things he had? He probably gets them for pennies on the dollar."

Sam just smiled at her. "Safeguards, remember? You going to put a price on that?"

She huffed out a breath. "No. But still, I—"

"If I end up dead, you can go back and get a refund." Sam fired up the truck. "Okay?"

Lacey stuck her tongue out at him.

When they pulled up to Pilar's, Ed's truck was not in evidence. Sam pulled close to the house, and Pilar came out the door to greet them. She hugged them each, and they were just walking toward the house when Ed drove up.

Lacey did not know Ed LaRosa well, but liked what she had seen. He seemed to be an even-handed stepfather to Kenzie and Daniel, and harbored no jealousy of Sam. He was a couple inches shorter than Sam, and a few pounds overweight, but had a ready smile which he flashed at Lacey.

Sam made the introductions and Ed and Pilar immediately got into a discussion in Spanish.

"She wants to know what she can do," Ed said.

Sam grabbed some tools and started toward the digging site. "Tell her to pray," he said.

They took all the tools and the cooler around the side of the house. Ed had his own landscaping business and had brought more shovels, a caliche bar and another pickaxe. Lacey thought it looked like they were going to dig to China.

"The steps start here," Sam said, toeing the ground where he had dug before. "They seem to angle down parallel to the side of the house, so at least we shouldn't have to dig around any foundations. The ground is dry, but not too hard."

Ed immediately hefted a pickaxe and used the point to scratch dirt away from the bit of exposed wood.

"First," Sam said, "a few precautions." He held the paper bag. Reaching inside, he pulled out sprigs of herbs and passed one to each of them. "Put this in a pocket or somewhere," he said. Lacey tucked hers in the watch pocket of her jeans. Sam stuck his in his hair just above his ponytail. Lacey stifled a laugh.

"What?" he challenged.

"Doesn't quite have the same effect as an eagle feather," she said.

Sam gave her a lopsided grin. "And now these," he said, passing an obsidian mirror to each. "Hang 'em around your necks."

"What do these do?" Lacey asked.

"They reflect the evil back to its origin," he said.

They each slipped a string necklace over their head, the polished slice of stone hanging heavy below each throat. Lacey liked the fact that the obsidian rested just above her heart.

She wasn't sure if she felt better or worse that Pilar was adorning herself with the protections as well.

"If anyone starts to feel anything unusual, any symptoms of sickness, shortness of breath—anything—stop and get away. Don't ignore it." Sam stared meaningfully at Ed and Lacey. "Got it?"

They both nodded.

"Okay." Sam picked up a pickaxe. "Lace, why don't you and Pilar stand back a bit while we break ground?"

Lacey put a hand to Pilar's back and guided the old woman into the shade against the wall of the house. She pulled the cooler over and patted the flat top of it.

"Sit?" she asked Pilar, motioning to the cooler.

"No," Pilar said. Instead, she turned toward the front of the house and waved to Lacey to follow. The two of them went inside and Pilar pulled a folding chair from a corner of the kitchen. Lacey grabbed three more, and they brought them out and set them near the cooler.

She and Pilar took their seats as the men attacked the hard ground.

They actually made good progress. The pickaxes split great chunks of earth away from the packed ground, and before long Sam grabbed a shovel and was heaving big pieces aside. They found the full width of the top stair, the wood dry and crumbling.

Lacey had to remind herself to breathe. She alternated between holding her breath at every new impact of the pickaxe and monitoring her own body for any sensations of ghostly attack. She also kept a sharp eye on Sam and Ed, watching their faces, their demeanor and coloring. She stayed alert to anything that might indicate Reyes' displeasure.

"Got something," Sam said suddenly. He brought out a shovelful of dirt for all to see. Stained the same color as the ground was a large round pod, its skin bristling with short pointed spikes. A split in the pod revealed small black seeds.

"Datura," Ed said. "It's a hallucinogen." He picked it up and held it for Pilar to see. "*Brujo*?" he asked.

Pilar nodded. "*Brujo, si.*"

"Witchcraft," Ed told Sam and Lacey.

Sam had an idea. "Would you ask Pilar if she's got a small box, something we can put stuff like this in?"

Ed did. Pilar disappeared back into the house and returned with an open cardboard box. Sam laid the datura pod inside, then continued digging.

Lacey grabbed a shovel and began moving the mounting pile of dirt further from the hole. The obsidian mirror thudded against her chest with the repetitive motion, each contact providing some comfort.

All of a sudden a dust devil whirled up from nowhere and spun wildly across the hole. The loose dirt spiraled up easily into a fierce funnel and pelted Sam, Ed and Lacey. They all dropped their tools and threw their arms up across their faces.

"Ow!" Lacey said as the grit pelted her face. She was instantly sorry; dirt invaded her mouth, the earthy taste thick on her tongue. She dared not try to spit it out. Instead she clamped her mouth shut and tried not to swallow.

The dust devil flailed at them mercilessly, small rocks and weeds pocking the wall of the house. The wind grabbed at any loose clothing, tugging on sleeves and pant legs. Sam's ponytail fluttered like a flag in a gale, the black strands tangling around his face.

No one spoke. No one moved. They just planted their feet and stood firm against the onslaught.

Fingers of wind tugged at Lacey's obsidian mirror.

Finally, after several interminable minutes, the dust devil gave up. It weakened, its whirling force flagging. The brown cloud of dust and dirt began to fall apart, and then, as quickly as it started, it disappeared.

Lacey peeked out around her crossed arms cautiously. There was not a breath of wind. The trees across the street at the mission showed not a leaf moving.

She pulled her arms away and spat dirt from her mouth.

"You okay?" Sam asked.

"Yeah." She spit again. "Holy crap, what was that?" She glanced over at Pilar. Luckily the old woman had sheltered against the wall and had escaped the brunt of the wind.

"*Brujo,*" she said.

Lacey nodded. "Yeah. *Brujo.*"

They continued digging, but not without keeping an eye out for other manifestations. At one point a cloud drifted across the sun, and Lacey glanced around worriedly at the sudden darkness.

The cloud passed without incidence.

They found more flakes of obsidian. They had five steps uncovered when they found another datura pod. One by one, Sam tossed the artifacts into the box. The number was growing.

Lacey stopped to get a drink of water and wipe the sweat from her face when she heard a weird *thunk* from the dig. Both Sam and Ed were in the hole. Lacey saw Sam lift up the shovel and jam it down again, point first.

Thunk.

She was just about to ask about it when the dust devil returned. The mini-tornado spun madly across the ground, flinging rocks and dirt and debris in a furious eddy. It pelted them all, and the house, in a hail of small rocks. Lacey tossed down her water bottle and spread-eagled her body over Pilar, her hands flat against the house. Arched over the old woman, she couldn't shield her own face but could only duck her head, and she felt the whirling grit scratch her cheeks and forehead. The wind buffeted her body, blew her hair all about her face in a wild tangle, and ripped the obsidian mirror from her neck.

She wanted to cry out, wanted to grab for the mirror, wanted to fall to the ground in a ball. She did none of those. She pressed her hands more firmly against the wall, set her feet solidly against the ground and squeezed her eyes and mouth shut. The dust devil beat her with its tightly coiled winds, like the revolving brush in a car wash, hammering her body, pulling her hair, howling in her ears.

Please, she begged silently, *please, please, please, go away. Go away.*

A cramp grabbed her calf muscle. She pushed harder against the ground to fight the pain. She grimaced, and immediately dirt coated her lips.

Then, with a shriek, it was gone. The wind died in an instant, the dirt and small rocks only filtering down to the ground after the fact.

The air was deathly still.

Lacey pushed herself away from the wall and felt a loose coating of dirt fall from her arms. She backed away from Pilar and shook her body, brushing dirt from her clothes and hair. She dragged a hand across her mouth, then touched Pilar's shoulder.

"You okay?" she asked. "Okay?"

"*Sí*." Pilar's voice croaked. The old woman dusted herself off, but seemed unharmed. Lacey got a fresh bottle of water from the cooler and handed it to her.

"*Gracias*," Pilar said.

"You guys okay?" Lacey called to the men. They'd hunkered down in the hole, and only now straightened up. They were both coated with dirt. Lacey brought water for both of them.

"Yeah," Sam said. "Thanks." He took a bottle and cracked the seal, taking a big drink. Ed did the same.

Lacey found her mirror on the ground; the string was gone. She pulled the stone from the dirt and slipped it into her pocket.

"I don't know what you found down there," she said, "but I'd bet dollars to doughnuts Reyes is not happy about it."

Sam grinned at her, his teeth gritty. "You think?" He gulped another mouthful of water and handed the bottle back to Lacey. "Come on. Let's see what we got."

They cleared the dirt away and found a flat surface of metal. Old metal. A battered, black trunk with reinforced corners and a large, pitted hasp. They dug carefully around all four sides and found an ancient padlock through the hasp. Sam crashed the point of his shovel into the padlock, and the old rusty metal parted.

Slowly, cautiously, he lifted the lid.

~~~

FOURTEEN

"What's in there?" Lacey stood at the edge of the hole and peered down into the dim interior of the trunk. "Looks like burlap."

"Maybe sack cloth," Ed said.

Sam hunkered down next to the trunk. "Lacey," he said, "hand me one of those trowels, would you?"

Lacey found a trowel and passed it down. Sam used it to carefully delve into the folds of fabric. He pulled one section back, stared down into the shadows, and sighed.

"Better call the police," he told Lacey.

"Why?"

He looked up at her. "There's a body in here."

Lacey pulled her phone from her pocket and came around to the stairs. "Let me see. I'll take some pictures." She descended the stairs carefully. Between the rotting wood and the scatter of small rocks, the footing was dicey.

Ed stepped aside so Lacey could get close to the trunk. She snapped a picture of it in the confines of the hole, then moved closer. Sam, using the trowel, pulled aside a fold of cloth so she could see underneath.

It was a head—a skull mostly, although some skin was still attached. A few matted wisps of hair were evident. The skull and skin were the same color as the ground, all of it a medium brown.

Lacey snapped more pictures.

"Can you pull the material back a little more?" she asked Sam.

He repositioned the trowel and slid it underneath another fold of fabric. Being careful not to touch anything with his own hands, he pushed aside the material and revealed more of the body.

Lacey looked closer. "What is that?" She pointed, almost gagging.

Sam examined the face. "It looks," he said, "like the mouth was sewn shut."

~~~

A half hour later, Lacey sat beside Pilar in one of the folding chairs in the shade and sipped her water. Sam, Ed and two policemen were all down in the hole, staring at the body in the trunk as they waited for homicide detectives to show up.

Lacey leaned her head back against the wall and sighed. She tried not to think of those dark threads crisscrossing the seam of the ancient mouth, piercing the dry, leathery skin. A chill shivered up her spine.

Pilar said something, and when Lacey looked over, she saw the old woman was offering a handkerchief. Lacey questioned her with her eyes, and Pilar pantomimed wiping her own face with the cloth. Lacey took the thin, white kerchief and dabbed at her face. The cloth showed small specks of blood.

Oh, yeah, she thought. The pelting of rocks by the dust devil. She'd forgotten all about that. She poured some of her water on the kerchief and dabbed again at her cheeks, neck and forehead. The small flecks of blood mingled with larger smears of dirt.

A second police car pulled up, this one unmarked, and parked beside the first cruiser. Two men in suits walked up.

One flashed a badge. "Where—?"

"That way," Lacey said, pointing to the hole. She was too tired to offer more. She laid her head back again, took a sip of water and pressed the cool bottle to her cheek.

It didn't take too long before one of the detectives climbed out of the hole and approached Lacey and Pilar.

"I'm Detective Ronson," he said. He had a pen and a notepad. "Could I get your names, please?"

"I'm Lacey Fitzpatrick, and this is Pilar Archuleta."

"You're the homeowner?" Ronson asked.

Lacey waved her bottle at Pilar. "She is. She doesn't speak English."

Ronson frowned. "Can you tell me why you were digging here? What led up to this… discovery?"

"Sure," Lacey said. She pointed to another chair. "Have a seat. This might take a while."

Three hours later, Sam pulled his truck into the parking lot at Lacey's apartment. Instead of just letting her out as she might have expected, he pulled into a parking spot and shut down the truck.

"Invite me in," he said.

Lacey stared at him. He knew he didn't need an invitation. The look in his eyes got her attention, though.

"Sure. Come on in."

They hadn't talked all the way back. Lacey felt dopey. The events of the morning, then those burros that Pilar had fixed for them—meat, beans and cheese in homemade tortillas—combined with the repetitive, and disbelieving, questions by the homicide detectives had dulled her brain. Her arms felt heavy and she had to will herself to get out of the truck.

Inside the apartment, she grabbed two Gatorades out of the fridge and handed one to Sam. They gravitated to the couch. Sam sat down and put his arm out; Lacey crawled under it and rested her head on his chest.

"We did good today," he said in a low voice. "That was one of the other spirits I felt there at Pilar's. That was the one I said was imprisoned."

"Do you know who he is?" Lacey asked.

"No. A priest by the look of the old robes. But beyond that, no."

She nodded. "Could the detectives tell cause of death?" If the body had had its aorta ripped in half, would there be enough evidence of soft tissue to tell? The body was pretty well desiccated.

"Probably suffocation," Sam said. "The hands were tied behind the back, but there was evidence he was still alive when he was buried."

"Ugh," she groaned. A thought occurred to her. "Could a ghost do that? Put someone in a trunk and bury them?"

"No. That man was killed while Reyes was still alive."

That made her sit up. "So if we can find out who he is and when he died…"

"We'll know when Reyes lived. This could be the key to finding out who Reyes really is. And maybe what happened to him to turn him into such a monster."

She settled against Sam again. "So let me see if I understand this. Finding this body doesn't get rid of Reyes."

He didn't answer right away. "I don't think so. We'll find out from Pilar in a day or two, but I don't think so."

She yawned. "Yeah, probably not. Jeez, I am toast. I need to take a shower, get all this grit off of me. But I'm too tired to move."

"Relax," Sam said. He pulled her closer. "There's nothing else we have to do today."

She leaned into him. "What about the kids?" she asked. "Aren't you supposed to pick them up for the weekend?"

"I called Christine," he said. "I'll get them later, maybe before dinner."

"Oh, okay. Good." She snuggled in, pillowing her head on his chest. "I'm so tired." Her voice was muffled by her mouth against his shirt.

"I know," he said. "Go ahead; get some sleep."

"Maybe, just a little," she said. "Just a little…"

~~~

FIFTEEN

Wednesday afternoon, they reconvened in the director's office with Swayze and Father David. Swayze had copies of the police report for Lacey and Sam. Father David had already been apprised.

Lacey scanned the report. Male, thirty to forty years of age; cause of death undetermined but asphyxiation likely. Not much they didn't already know.

She looked up at the director. "Do they know who he is?"

Swayze shook his head. "They don't have any records of a priest disappearing, at least not in the last sixty or seventy years."

"It's that old?" she asked.

"Older," Father David said. "We believe his name is Father Timoteo de la Varga. He disappeared from the mission in 1900. There was speculation that he might have left the priesthood, just... walked away. He was never heard from again."

Lacey stared down at the brief police report. "That's all?" she asked. "That's all anyone knows?"

The director shrugged. "A hundred and seventeen years ago? There aren't many records that far back. Just names and dates, I'm afraid."

Lacey frowned. Names and dates didn't cut it. They needed history. Stories. She turned toward Father David.

"Do you know of any really old people associated with the mission? People who worked here for a long time?"

Father David seemed surprised at the question. "Uh, I don't know. There might be some…"

"If there's no written history, there could still be some oral history," she said. "Stories passed down from one generation to the next. Hidden stories, not part of the mainstream history."

The priest nodded. "Yes, I understand. History not… sanctioned."

"Exactly," Lacey said. She arched an eyebrow at him.

Father David looked to the director. Swayze nodded.

"All right," the priest said. "Let me, uh, look into it. I may know someone."

"Great." Lacey sat back in her chair.

"But finding this body hasn't changed anything?" Swayze asked. He put his question to Sam.

"We're not entirely sure," Sam said carefully. "Pilar says there's still a presence there, although it seems to be... reduced somewhat. I would guess that Reyes was drawing power from the spirit of the imprisoned priest, and now that we've freed him, so to speak, Reyes has less to draw on. But he's still there." He turned to Father David. "Once the police release the body, will the priest get an ordained burial?"

Father David glanced at Swayze. "We can do that, certainly," he said. Swayze nodded.

"Good. That should lay the priest to rest. Literally." Sam sighed. "He's been in anguish a long time."

Father David stared at Sam thoughtfully.

Lacey flipped through the police report one more time. "Then I guess that's all for now," she said. She glanced at each man in turn, checking for input. No one had any more to offer.

"All right." She folded the report and tucked it into her pack. "Father David, if you'll let me know as soon as you find an elder I can talk to, I'd appreciate it."

"Yes, of course," he said. "I'll get right on it."

~~~

Lacey was quiet on the drive home, her brain awhirl. What else could they do?

"Hey," she said suddenly to Sam. "You know what you said about releasing that old priest, and that Reyes can't draw on his energy anymore?"

"Yeah." Sam turned toward her in his seat, his interest piqued.

"Earlier you said there were several other entities there, right?"

"Right."

"Any ideas who? Or what their story is?"

Sam thought back. "All the energies felt male, the good and the bad. But beyond that, no. What are you thinking?"

"I'm wondering," she said, "if they might be Pilar's father and husband. Both men were killed by Reyes' psychic surgery. For all we know, they may have died right there in that house. Do you think that he was somehow able to tie them up psychically, so he could draw power from them, too? Even if their bodies were buried in a proper graveyard?"

The light in Sam's eyes spoke of his excitement. "Yes! That could definitely happen." He mulled that over. "What we'd need to do is a releasement for those two men. If we could free them, we'd weaken Reyes even more." He smiled at Lacey.

"Good job, partner. You're starting to think like a medium."

Lacey laughed. "Heaven help us," she said. "We're going to get this son of a bitch."

~~~

Melissa Bowersock

SIXTEEN

Thursday afternoon Father David called Lacey with a name.

"Jerome Pequeño," he said. "He worked at the mission for almost fifty years." He gave her the number.

"Was he a priest?"

"No. His father was, but his mother was a Juaneño, so there was some, uh…"

"Discrimination?" Lacey provided.

Father David sighed. "Yes, I'm afraid so. Mestizos were not considered to be good… material for the priesthood back then. Jerome worked as a maintenance man."

"How old is he?" Lacey asked.

"Ninety-two."

"Jeez. Is he pretty sharp? Still clear-minded?"

"I think so. At least that was the impression I got when I talked to him."

"Does he understand what this is all about? What we're doing?"

"Yes. I told him. He was hesitant at first, but then seemed to warm to it. I think if anyone knows anything, it'll be him."

"Okay, great. I'll call him," Lacey said. "Thanks."

She called Sam and told him. "Do you want to be there when I interview him?"

There was silence for a moment; Lacey recognized Sam's thorough consideration. "No. You go ahead. If you can meet with him tomorrow, that would be great. I'm hoping we can do the releasement on Saturday morning. Keep chipping away at Reyes as much as possible, keep him scrambling."

"You and Ed arranging that?"

"Yeah. After the dig, Ed's all in on this, and he and Pilar get along great."

"Okay," Lacey said. "Sounds like a plan. I'll call you when I have something to report, and you can call me when you've got things set for Saturday."

"Deal."

Lacey was able to set up her interview with Jerome for Friday afternoon. He lived with his daughter and her husband in a middle-class neighborhood some distance from the mission. Lacey drove over and was met by the daughter at the door.

"Mrs. Sandoval?" she asked. "I'm Lacey Fitzpatrick. We spoke on the phone."

"Yes, come in." She pulled the door open wide and let Lacey in. She looked to be in her early sixties, neat and trim, her dark hair only minimally shot through with gray strands. "You're from the mission, right?" she asked. Lacey thought she detected some uneasiness in the woman.

"I'm a private investigator, hired by the mission," Lacey said. "My partner and I found an old burial across the street from the mission, and we're trying to identify the body. There are no records to substantiate it."

"Oh." Lena Sandoval looked partly mollified, but partly not. "I'm still not sure I understand…"

Lacey smiled. "Because there are no official records, we're turning to elders who might have heard stories. Rumors that might have survived. From what I understand, your father worked at the mission for a long time."

"Yes," Lena said, sounding somewhat more satisfied. "Come on in here." She led Lacey into the living room. "Dad, Lacey Fitzpatrick is here."

The old man looked tiny in the oversized recliner. He was thin and frail, his mostly bald head dotted with tufts of wispy hair and age spots. His eyes looked huge behind thick glasses, but they gleamed with interest.

"Hello," Lacey said, crossing to him. She put out her hand and pressed his warmly. "Thank you for seeing me, Mr. Pequeño."

"Yes," he said, his voice thin and reedy. "Please, sit down."

Lacey took the chair across a small end table from him and set her pack on the floor. She got out her notebook and a pen.

She noticed Lena hovering behind her father.

"I believe Father David told you a little about what we're doing," Lacey started. "And I understand your family has a long-time connection to the mission. Your father was a priest there?"

"Yes, that's right."

"What was his name?"

"Joseph Fidelio Pequeño."

"What year was he born?" Lacey asked.

"Eighteen ninety-five."

She noticed Lena getting restless. Lacey had purposely started with very benign questions—names and dates—hoping the woman would get bored and find something else to do. She'd rather not have an audience once she got into the real purpose of the interview.

Lena shifted behind her father. "Uh, do you want something to drink? Water or anything?"

"Thanks, no," Lacey said. "I'm fine."

Lena nodded and took that opportunity to leave them.

Lacey waited until she disappeared down a hall, then returned her attention to the old man.

"Did Father David tell you about the burial we found? The body of the old priest?"

"Yes," Jerome said. His thin voice didn't carry. Lacey had to lean closer to hear him.

"We believe it's the body of Father Timoteo de la Varga, who disappeared in 1900. Now since your father was born in 1895, obviously the disappearance was before his time as a priest, but I'm wondering if he might have heard about it and, possibly, passed the story down to you."

Jerome studied Lacey for a moment, those milky eyes evaluating her. She returned his stare with her own, direct and open, patient and welcoming.

"You're here about the ghosts," he said abruptly.

Lacey nodded, surprised he'd made that leap. "Yes, actually, I am," she affirmed. "The mission called my partner and me in to see if we could dispel them." She lowered her voice. "Did you ever have an… experience during your time there?"

Jerome smiled, but he fidgeted a little with his hands. The gnarled old fingers clasped and unclasped the knees of his baggy trousers. He glanced over his shoulder. His daughter was nowhere in sight. "Those who have not felt it do not believe," he said quietly.

"Have you felt it?"

"Oh, yes," he said. "Many times."

"What kind of experiences did you have?" she asked.

"Hands," he said.

"Hands?"

He nodded. "Cold hands. On my shoulder, on my neck. He would come up behind me, when I was working. I learned to never turn my back to the east."

"Did he ever hurt you?" Lacey asked softly.

"No. I didn't stay around. If he was there, I left the area. Sometimes I would work out there and not feel him, but if he came, I left."

Lacey jotted a few notes.

"He hated priests."

She glanced up. "Do you know why?"

"The story my father told me," he said, "was that his wife was ill. She'd been going to a *curandera*. Do you know what that is?"

"A healer," Lacey said.

"Yes. Her progress had been very slow. She went to a priest and asked what else she might do. He told her to abandon the native ways and turn to Christ. To throw away all the old charms. He said the only way back to health was through the church. She believed him."

He paused, his eyes hard. "She died."

Lacey swallowed. "So that's why…"

He nodded. "Yes. He blamed the priest for her death. And swore revenge."

"Was that priest… de la Varga?"

"Yes. It was not long after that when the priest disappeared. Some said he left, perhaps ran away because he feared for his life. Some felt he'd been killed. No one could prove it." He shrugged. "They didn't try very hard. No one wanted to anger the *brujo.*"

"Did Father David tell you how we found the body?" she asked.

He shook his head.

"Buried in a trunk. His hands tied behind his back. His mouth sewn shut. He was buried alive."

Jerome took that in. His eyes drifted away from Lacey for a moment. She wondered if he were realizing how lucky he'd been to escape harm.

"Mr. Pequeño," she said softly, drawing him back. "Do you know who the man was? The *brujo*?"

He returned his gaze to her, his mouth pressed into a thin line. "Yes."

She waited, wondering if he were afraid to say the name. She pleaded with her eyes.

"Guillermo Casales."

~~~

SEVENTEEN

On the drive back home, Lacey had to force herself to watch the road, to stay present and cognizant of the traffic.

But her mind churned.

Guillermo Casales. Pilar's grandfather. He'd killed the priest while he was alive, then had killed his own son and granddaughter's husband while dead.

It was very probable, she thought, that those two had gone up against Reyes, had tried to eradicate him.

And failed. Tragically.

There had been an earlier effort to drive him out years before, Jerome said. The house had been burned to the ground. On purpose. No doubt the place had been consecrated in some manner, cleansed, blessed.

It hadn't worked.

Perhaps Humberto had built the new house hoping it was safe, only to find out he was wrong. It was, after all, the family home. She wondered if he had felt the obligation to keep Reyes contained with spells and charms, as Pilar did now. Or if he had made one last-ditch effort to drive him out with a crucifix and had paid for it with his life.

She shook her head, glanced around to reacquaint herself with the freeway she drove. Distracted driving was not good. And she was definitely distracted. Luckily she was almost home.

As she pulled off the freeway at her exit, she wondered if Pilar knew who Reyes was. No, she would have told them. Wouldn't she? How would she feel when she found out? Lacey tried to imagine being told her very own grandfather was a witch, the man who had loved to play solitaire and go bird-watching and had built her a doll house when she was little. Impossible.

Would Pilar think so? Or would she take it in stride? She was used to so many impossible things.

Lacey pulled into the parking lot and guided her car into her numbered slot. First thing she had to do was call Sam.

Entering her apartment and tossing her pack down, she grabbed her phone and checked the time. Almost five. Sam would be home.

"I was just going to call you," he said. "We're all set for tomorrow. Pick me up at eight-thirty?"

"Sure," she said. She flopped down on the couch.

"You find out anything?" he asked.

She laughed grimly. "Oh, yeah."

He listened in silence while she told him the story.

"Holy cow," he said. "Her own grandfather?"

"Yup. I just wonder how she's going to take that."

Sam considered that. "I actually think she'll do okay with it. I mean, not *okay* okay, but I think she'll understand."

"Well, it all certainly makes sense when you know the whole story," she said.

He agreed. "I'm glad we're doing the releasement tomorrow," he said. "At least she'll know her father and husband will be free. That's two positives against the negative."

"Yeah." She blew out a breath. "I just hope it's enough."

"Me, too," he said in a low tone. "Me, too."

~~~

Melissa Bowersock

EIGHTEEN

They arrived to find Ed already there, deep in conversation with Pilar beside his truck. Lacey pulled up next to it, and she and Sam joined the other two.

Pilar gave both Sam and Lacey a hug. Her eyes looked suspiciously moist.

"She knows what we're doing?" Lacey asked Ed softly.

"Yeah. She says it's time."

Lacey nodded. She glanced at Sam. "It's your show."

"Actually," he said, heading for the house, "it's mine and Pilar's. Come on."

Lacey had seen the paper bag Sam brought. She wondered if he had more herbs, more charms. But when they all stopped around the table inside, he dumped out a fat smudge stick and a baggie of small black seeds.

Pilar carried over a footed brass vase that was half filled with sand. In her other hand, she had several sticks of incense. She laid all that on the table, then retrieved two framed pictures of Hispanic men.

"*Padre?*" Lacey asked, pointing to the image of the older man.

"*Si,*" Pilar said. "*Y mi esposo.*" She caressed the face of the younger man with a loving fingertip.

Lacey looked to Sam. "What are we doing?"

"First," Sam said, "we're going to purify." He grinned at Lacey. "This is going to be a multi-denominational ceremony."

Multi-denominational is right, she thought. Navajo, Catholic and Acjehemen, plus a little witchcraft thrown in for good measure. She recognized the datura seeds.

Sam lit his smudge stick, turning the wrapped bundle reverently in the flame of the lighter, blowing on it softly until the plant material caught the flame. It flared slightly, then settled into a smolder. The blue smoke began to rise.

Then he passed the lighter to Pilar. She pushed several sticks of incense into the sand in the vase and lit them. Soon the stronger scent of incense mingled with the fresh smell of cedar, all rising up toward the ceiling.

Sam began a slow walk through the house. He bathed the corners and walls with smoke, covering both the front room and the bedroom. Pilar followed behind with her incense. While Sam was silent and focused, Pilar spoke softly, reverently, in a singsong, chanting voice.

They stopped at the closet door. Sam waved the smudge stick all across the face of the door, then stood aside for Pilar. She lifted the little vase in both hands, presenting it and the smoke. She spoke so softly Lacey couldn't catch any of the words.

When she stepped back and nodded to Sam, he pulled the door open and stepped inside. He waved his smudge stick carefully, avoiding the clothes that hung on the rod. He lifted the smoke up into the corners, pulled it across the floor, let it curl out the doorway.

Then Pilar took over. She did much the same with her incense, speaking softly the entire time. Finally she backed out of the closet and Sam closed the door.

"Outside?" he asked her, motioning with his hand. She nodded. They all trooped outside, Sam and Pilar in the lead, Lacey and Ed following.

Sam and Pilar walked the property, circling the little house and paying particular attention to the dig area roped off by yellow crime tape. Sam visited all four corners of the property, tossing a few datura seeds at the boundaries, while Pilar walked more slowly, staying closer to the house. The morning breeze caught the trails of fragrant smoke and pulled at them, diffusing both the smoke and the scents on the soft air.

Finally they all met in front of the house. Sam held his smudge stick so the blue smoke continued to spiral upward lazily, but Pilar set her incense on the ground. Several of the sticks were spent, but one or two continued to emit faint smoke.

Sam nodded to Pilar. She bowed her head for a moment, whispering softly to herself, her hands folded in prayer. Then she lifted her old gray head and raised her arms to the morning sun. In a singsong voice, she chanted to the east, turned and addressed the north, the west, the south, then returned to the east. She spread her arms wide and lifted her voice, pleading, extolling, releasing. Tears slipped down her wrinkled cheeks, and her voice broke, but she went on. Finally her arms gave out and dropped heavily to her sides. She whispered a last invocation—a goodbye—and bowed her head in silence once more.

They all stood very still. The only sound was an early morning car going down the street. Lacey wondered what a car was doing in a church.

Sam raised his smudge stick and offered it to the four directions as Pilar had. He wafted the smoke in a circle as he did so, and when he finally brought his arm down, he said simply to the quiet air, "Go in peace. Go with God."

Lacey wiped a tear from her eye and stood silently as Sam's words faded away.

Pilar nodded to herself, then rested a hand on Sam's arm. She patted his arm absently and took a step toward the house. She looked tired.

"I'll be right back," Sam said to Lacey and Ed, "then we can go."

Lacey went to her car and leaned against the side to wait. Ed joined her.

"Some morning, huh?" he asked.

Lacey smiled up at him weakly. "Yeah. Not your normal, everyday Saturday, is it?"

"Not my normal everyday week or month," he admitted.

Lacey laughed. "You've never seen Sam release souls before?"

He shook his head. "Nope. Heard about it, but never seen it. It's... something else."

"Yes, it is." She let out a deep breath. "I just hope this does it. We'll have to see—"

Suddenly she heard a squawk from Pilar and glanced toward the house. Sam was on the ground, struggling. Pilar began to scream, not in fear, but railing, railing against something—or someone. She tugged at Sam, trying to get him up, trying to help, but she was too weak to have any effect.

Sam clutched at his chest.

~~~

NINETEEN

"Oh, Jesus!" Lacey said. She pushed away from the car and grabbed Ed's hand on her way by. "Come on! We've got to get him away from here. Sam!"

She ran to him and dropped to the ground, then wondered frantically what the hell to do first. Ed fell to Sam's other side and grabbed his arm.

"Help me pull him up!" he said.

Lacey grabbed his other arm and clamped both hands around his bicep. Together she and Ed pulled him into a sitting position, no small feat with his thrashing and flailing.

"Sam!" she called. "Come on! Get to your feet. Get away from here!"

He continued to flail, his fingers clutching his throat, his chest, as if trying to grasp invisible hands. His eyes were wide, his face drained of all color.

"Pull!" Ed yelled. "Pull hard! Now!"

He and Lacey pulled together, yanking Sam unsteadily to his feet. Ed didn't wait. "Okay, come on! Run!"

The three of them took off running across the bare ground, past the vehicles, past the sidewalk, into the street. Lacey only barely glanced around for cars, but thankfully there were none. All she knew was that she had to keep her grip on Sam's arm, and they had to get to the mission grounds.

They gained the far sidewalk, Lacey and Ed pulling Sam up the curb in silent unity. The driveway was not far. They ran flat out, dragging Sam, and tore inside the opening in the wall. Together the three of them headed for a patch of green lawn, and fell gratefully onto the cool grass in a heap.

Lacey checked Sam. He was breathing hard, his mouth open, but his hands were at his sides. Gently she moved her fingers over the skin of his throat and down inside the neck of his t-shirt, feeling for any break in the skin, any swelling or edema. She felt none, but checked again anyway.

"I'm okay," he panted. He took her hand and squeezed it. "I'm okay."

"Are you sure?" she asked. His color was coming back slowly, and he was regaining his breath, but she still didn't trust his assessment. "We should get you to a doctor," she said.

He shook his head and pushed himself up into a sitting position. "No. I'm okay. Really." He leaned forward over his bent knees and dragged in several deep breaths.

"I'll go find you some water," Ed said. He scrambled to his feet and headed for the door.

Lacey scooted as close to Sam as she could get and rubbed his back gently. He met her worried gaze and smiled.

"That was him," she said.

He nodded, still catching his breath. "Yeah. He's not happy."

Lacey snorted. "Really? I couldn't tell."

Sam crossed his legs, Indian-style, and leaned toward her. "He's desperate. He's lost a lot of his power and he's panicking. That's a good sign."

Lacey considered that. "But he's still strong enough to try to kill you."

Sam nodded. "Yeah. I noticed that."

Ed returned with a bottle of water and handed it to Sam, then took a seat on the grass. Sam chugged the water gratefully.

"Thanks," he said. He drank nearly half the bottle, then offered it to the other two. Lacey took a sip.

"What about Pilar?" he asked. "Is she okay?"

Lacey glanced out the driveway, but couldn't see the house from their vantage point. "I don't know. All I could think about was getting you out of there."

"Let me go look," Ed said.

Lacey put a hand on his arm. "Be careful," she said.

"I will."

He walked to the sidewalk and stared across the street. Lacey saw him raise a hand and wave.

"She's okay," he said when he returned. "Still standing."

"Good," Sam said. He took another swallow of water and pushed himself to his feet. Lacey stood with him.

"I'll go get the car and bring it over here," she said. "Then I'll bring Ed's truck." She arched an eyebrow at both men. "You guys stay here."

She thought Sam might argue. He seemed about to say something, but didn't. Finally he nodded. "Okay. Just be careful."

"Don't worry about that," she muttered.

Once she'd checked on Pilar and then brought the two vehicles over one by one, Lacey insisted Sam sit in her car. She and Ed leaned against the side and the three of them took stock.

"Obviously," Sam said, "we're not done yet." He glanced meaningfully at Lacey.

"Yeah, I get that," she said. She crossed her arms over her chest. "So what do we need to do? How do we get rid of him for good?"

Sam stared down at the ground. No answers seemed forthcoming.

"It sounds like Pilar's done everything she knows and it wasn't enough," Lacey said. "We've taken away everything that he's used to gain power, but he's still here." She shook her head. "What's left? How do you kill someone who's already dead?"

Sam raised his eyes to her. His look hardened. "I don't know," he said grimly. "I honestly don't know."

~~~

TWENTY

Lacey did a lot of pacing that weekend. She'd sit at the computer for a half hour or so, researching ghosts, demons, ancient legends and superstitions, then she'd vault to her feet and pace. She'd walk a pattern—dining room to living room to kitchen, back to dining room—then sit and search again. Evil, magic, witchcraft, exorcisms. Then she'd pace some more.

Nothing lit up in her mind, nothing brought that *ah ha* moment when it all became clear. She racked her brain for more topics, different ways of coming at the same problem, but nothing worked.

Nothing worked.

Her frustration mounted. How could they come so far and still have the same problem? They found the priest's body, they identified Reyes and his sources of psychic power, they released his victims, yet they still had him to contend with. It was as if they'd done nothing at all.

All their work to this point for nothing. It was maddening.

Several times she almost called Sam, but he'd have the kids and she knew venting to him would solve nothing more than passing her frustration to him. She was sure he had his own.

That was the scary part. Always before, Sam had the answers. He knew, or intuited, how to deal with the spirits they encountered. He knew what was necessary to break their hold on the physical world, to nudge them along on their spiritual journey toward wholeness, toward redemption.

But not this time.

She stared at her laptop, or out the window. There had to be a way to fight Reyes. Evil couldn't win.

Could it?

Monday morning, she called the director and reported their progress—and their brick wall.

"So you don't think you can get rid of him?" Swayze asked.

"We're still working on it," Lacey said. She couldn't admit defeat. Not yet. "Sam's working on it. We'll do all we can."

"I don't have to tell you how… disturbing it would be to know he's still there, still able to prey on people. If he's still powerful enough to attack…"

"Yes, sir, I know," she said. "I promise you, we're not giving up. We'll figure out a way." She hoped her words didn't sound as hollow as they felt to her.

"I hope so," Swayze said. "Perhaps Father David..." he offered.

"We'll see," she said. "If we need him, we'll definitely call. We'll keep working on it."

"All right." Swayze sighed. "Thanks, Lacey. Keep me posted."

"Yes, sir."

She keyed off the call and tossed the phone down glumly.

What else? What else?

No answers came.

Later that afternoon, her phone chimed. She checked the screen: Sam. Hope soared in her. Maybe he'd thought of something.

"Hi," she said, feeling more cheerful than she had all day.

"Hi. What are you doing?"

She sighed. "Not much. Thinking, researching, wishing, hoping. Not necessarily in that order."

"So you need a break," he said. "How about you come over here to my place? I just picked up some Chinese take-out."

"Really?" She sat up.

"Yeah. Come on over." He paused. "I called in the cavalry."

"The cavalry?" She had no idea what he was talking about.

"Yeah. Come on. Get your butt over here before the fried rice gets cold."

She was already grabbing her car keys. "Be there in twenty."

She pulled up next to the truck and parked. The drapes were pulled across the front window, giving her no clue as to who—or what—the cavalry might be. She knocked lightly on the door.

"Come on in," Sam's voice called from inside.

She pushed the door open and walked in. Sam was in the kitchen, but he wasn't alone. A small figure stood behind him.

She recognized that gray hair, pulled back into the traditional Navajo bun. She recognized that faded plaid flannel shirt. And she recognized that sun-browned face, skin like leather except where it crinkled around his eyes.

"Ben!" She ran to hug Sam's grandfather. The old man grinned happily and hugged her back. He felt small and frail inside the flannel shirt.

"Lacey," he said in his soft airy voice. "Good to see you."

"It's great to see you, too," she said, still dumbfounded. "I just can't believe you're here. I didn't think anything would get you off the reservation."

He smiled and tapped his temple. "Sam needs my ideas," he said.

Lacey turned to Sam. "This is the cavalry?" she asked.

"Yup." He arched an eyebrow at her. "Didn't think they had a Navajo regiment, did you?"

She couldn't help but laugh. This was too crazy, but maybe just what they needed. After all, Ben had helped them with the shapeshifter witch on the reservation some months ago.

"Okay, what can I do?" she asked, noting Sam had dumped cartons of food into bowls.

"Why don't you grab plates and silverware?" he said. "We'll eat in the living room."

They settled around the coffee table, much as Sam did with his kids. She liked the informality. Sam took a side chair and let Lacey and Ben share the couch.

There was something surreal about watching the eighty-four-year-old Navajo eating Chinese food.

"So, what?" she asked Sam. "You drove over and got him? He didn't fly." She felt certain of that.

"Yeah, I drove over yesterday, drove back today. I was getting absolutely nowhere on my own. I knew I needed help."

Lacey nodded, watching Ben inspect his sweet and sour chicken. He was such a gentle old soul. He took the chicken in his front teeth and chewed carefully, then smiled at the sweet taste and speared another piece with his fork.

"So Sam told you what we're up against?" she asked.

Ben pointed his fork at her full plate. "Eat first," he said.

She rolled her eyes playfully at Sam. "Okay, if you insist."

But she already felt more hopeful, and besides, the food tasted great.

By the time they'd cleared their plates and taken seconds—thirds, in Sam's case—and finished that, she felt pleasantly stuffed. She set her plate down and flopped back against the sofa cushions, moaning happily.

"Been skipping lunch?" Sam asked.

He knew her all too well. When she was worrying a problem like this one, she rarely took a proper break for food.

"Maybe," she admitted.

He nodded, knowing exactly what that meant. "You can give it a rest now. Ben's got ideas."

She turned toward the old one and watched him chase the last grains of fried rice around his plate with his fork.

He took his time. He finally wrangled the last wayward grain onto his fork and ate it, smiling contentedly at Lacey.

"You Fireclouds do this on purpose, don't you?" she fumed.

"Patience is a virtue," Sam said.

"Yeah, I know." She crossed her arms. "Okay, you let me know when you're ready to talk."

Both Sam and Ben set their finally empty plates on the table. Lacey pointedly ignored them.

"I told Ben about all we've done," Sam started. "All the progress we've made, and the stalemate we've got now."

Lacey sat up with interest.

"He's got some ideas," Sam finished. He motioned to his grandfather to take the floor.

Ben turned to Lacey and put his hand out toward her, fingers pointing upward, flat palm facing her. "Put your hand against mine," he said in his halting English. Lacey did so. "Now push."

She exerted mild pressure against his hand, just enough so he had to press back to keep his hand where it was. He held the balance for a moment, then suddenly pulled his hand away. Lacey's hand flailed in the empty air.

Ben grinned at her. "See?"

She crinkled her brow, frowning at him. "See what?"

"When you have resistance, you push against it. When resistance is gone..."

She was reminded of the old Zen Buddhist koan, *what is the sound of one hand clapping?* But she still wasn't clear on the application to Reyes.

"So you're saying we don't go up against him? We don't... confront him? Try to banish him?"

Ben nodded. "We don't fight him," he said.

Lacey glanced at Sam. He seemed to be okay with this, but she still wasn't sure she was getting it.

"Okay, what am I missing?" she asked. "If we don't fight him, he's free to go on terrorizing the neighborhood, even if it is in a diminished way."

Ben smiled at her and said something in Navajo, something she had no clue about.

That's helpful, she thought. She turned to Sam for a translation.

"Power and love cannot occupy the same space," he said.

Lacey blinked at him. *Were they both being obtuse on purpose? Or had they both lost their minds?*

"What?" she said. "We love him to death?"

"He brings power," Ben said. "We bring love."

Lacey stared at the old man. "How do we do that?" she asked.

He tapped his gray head, sat back against the cushions and smiled.

Lacey switched to Sam again. "He's working on it, right?" she offered hopefully.

"Yeah." Sam chuckled. "Not exactly what you were expecting, huh?"

"That's an understatement," she muttered.

"We're gonna hammer it out tonight. I'm hoping we can organize it for tomorrow or the next day. We'll just have to play it by ear."

"Yeah, but—" She was interrupted by the soft snoring from the corner of the couch. Ben, arms crossed, head down, slept peacefully.

Sam touched her arm. "He's tired," he said. "Come on." He got up and pulled Lacey with him. They went into the kitchen.

"Does he know what Reyes can do?" she hissed. "What he tried to do to you?"

"He does," Sam said in a quiet voice. "I told him."

"I don't mean to downplay Ben's wisdom," she said, "but I just want to be really sure he understands what's at stake. If we try something and it doesn't work—"

Sam silenced her with a kiss. He folded her into his arms and held her tightly, his mouth moving gently over hers.

When he pulled back, it took Lacey a minute to get her bearings.

"Are you trying to shut me up?" she asked, only half joking.

"I'm trying to tell you to not worry," he said. He cupped the side of her face in one hand. "We're going to do this. It'll be all right."

She wanted to believe him; she really did. But she couldn't throw all in, not yet. Instead, she agreed to go along—for now.

"Okay," she said. "I'm with you. But I'm still nervous."

He kissed her again. "Wanna spend the night? Maybe we could do something about those nerves." The look in his eyes made her heart flutter.

A sudden arrested snort from the living room broke the silence. Lacey slapped a hand over her mouth to stifle a laugh.

"Maybe not while you've got company," she said.

He angled his head at her. "Having the kids here never stopped you."

"Yeah, well…" She glanced toward the doorway. "This is a little different." She leaned up and kissed him. "When this is all over, we'll celebrate," she said.

He imprisoned her in his arms. "Promise?"

She smiled. "Oh, yeah. Promise."

"Okay," he said. "I'll hold you to it."

~~~

Melissa Bowersock

TWENTY-ONE

Tuesday was a nerve-racking day. She stared at her phone, sat next to it, carried it with her as she paced. She knew better than to call Sam; he would call when he and Ben were ready. But the silence was killing her.

She made a trip to the gym and worked out; no call.

She forced herself to eat lunch; no call.

She tried to read a book and threw it down in disgust.

No call.

Finally, at a quarter to six, it rang. She grabbed it.

"Sam?"

"I think we've got it," he said. "Can you meet us over at Ed and Christine's? Say about seven?"

"Sure. But is Ed—?"

"He wants to help. So does Christine. We'll hash it out there, okay?"

"Okay." She sighed, knowing she wouldn't get any more than that from him now. *Damned stoic Fireclouds.*

"See you then."

And he was gone.

She parked in front of the apartment building right behind Sam's truck. She'd been to the door of his ex's apartment before, but had never gone in. She shouldn't be nervous; she and Christine had met many times, and there had never been any issues. She crossed her fingers as she knocked on the door.

"Lacey," Ed said, pulling open the door. "Come on in." He gave her a quick hug.

"Lacey!" Kenzie ran to her for a welcome hug. Lacey stroked the shining black head. The girl was such a love bug.

"We're in here," Ed said, motioning toward the living room. Lacey followed, Kenzie stuck to her side.

The living room was primarily white and light blue with comfy overstuffed chairs and couch. It was a very welcoming space. Briefly Lacey wondered about the possibility of having a home like this, a home she and Sam could share. Could they ever do that? She nodded or waved to Christine, Daniel, Ben and Sam, and took the chair Sam vacated for her. He sat next to her on the arm, close enough to touch. Kenzie squirmed into the chair with her.

She knew better than to prompt the discussion.

"Okay, what we're doing here," Sam said, "is planning a ritual, a ceremony. Ben's working out the process, and he and Pilar will take point. The rest of us—we four"—he nodded to Lacey, Ed and Christine—"will bring all the loving energy we can manage. Together, we think the six of us can overpower Reyes."

Lacey glanced around nervously. She worried for the men. Sam and Ed both knew all too well the power of Reyes. Sam said Ben did, too. She and Christine and Pilar, she thought, were probably safe… but could they bank on that? Just because Reyes had never attacked a woman before, did that mean he couldn't change his tactics?

"And what exactly is the best way for us to do that?" she asked hesitantly.

Sam looked at Ben. "We've talked about singing, chanting, praying, using imagery and visualizations. Whatever we can do to fill our hearts, our minds, our souls, with love." He glanced around the room. "I know this is difficult. If I tell you not to think of a tiger, that's all you're going to think about. So if I tell you not to think about fear, it's hard to get away from it. But just remember: love and power cannot exist in the same place. It's important that we fill ourselves up with love, that we don't succumb to fear. We have to be ready for whatever Reyes throws at us, but we have to fill ourselves up with love so there's no room for anything else."

Lacey tried her best to project confidence, but she didn't feel it inside. What if she faltered and couldn't stay strong? What if she wavered, and her weakness imperiled all of them?

Sam put his hand on her shoulder, pulling her out of her fearful musings. He smiled at her.

"Ben and I have no doubt we can do this," he finished.

"Dad," Kenzie said, "I want to help, too. I love a lot of people." Lacey put her arm around the girl and hugged her.

"Me, too, Dad," Daniel said. "I can help, too."

Lacey looked up at Sam. *He wouldn't possibly consider this?* But he was looking very thoughtful.

"Yes, you can," he said finally. "You can both help us a lot. You'll stay here, but you'll also think about nothing but love, fill yourselves up with love for all of us, for our family. That will help us out tremendously. Think you can do that?"

Daniel groaned, no doubt recognizing the fact that he and his sister would be safely away from the danger. Kenzie watched her brother, uncertainty in her eyes.

Sam angled his head at his son, one dark eyebrow arched. "Daniel? You with us on this?"

Daniel scowled, but noted his father's insistence. He glanced at his sister and shrugged. "Yeah. We can do that."

Kenzie laughed, a sound of nervous relief. She glanced up at Lacey, and Lacey hugged her again.

"All right," Sam said. "Ben and I have talked about some visualizations we can use during the ceremony…"

~~~

TWENTY-TWO

It was all set. They would meet at Pilar's at five o'clock Wednesday afternoon. Ed and Christine would meet Lacey, Sam and Ben there.

Lacey was grateful for the daylight hour. They should have plenty of time to do this before dark set in, even in late October.

It was about the only thing she was grateful for.

Pilar, briefed in advance by Ed, welcomed them all. She seemed to recognize a kindred spirit in Ben, and he in her, even though they shared no language.

Lacey noted that the old woman seemed to show no trepidation at the upcoming ceremony. That was a good sign.

Sam and Ben walked the property while the rest of them waited together in the front yard. Ben walked silently, head down, while Sam occasionally said something to him in Navajo. They disappeared around the back of the house, and Lacey knew Sam was showing Ben the dig site.

When they rejoined the others, Ben looked resolute. He made suggestions for the ceremony and Ed translated for Pilar.

"We do it there," he said, waving a hand toward the dig site. Pilar agreed. "We form circle. Pilar is east. I am west. Others in between."

Lacey thought Pilar looked pleased to represent east, the rising sun. And humbled.

"We go," Ben said. He started around the side of the house. The rest followed.

Lacey noticed that everyone had a kerchief around their neck, as they'd discussed last night, and some were already pulling it up over their nose and mouth. She handed an extra to Pilar, who took it with an appreciative smile. It might be a small defense against Reyes' assault, but it would at least keep them from ingesting too much dirt if he called up a whirlwind.

She was surprised to see that the hole had been backfilled and the crime tape was gone. Apparently the physical investigation of the site was complete. But the location was clear. The recently disturbed earth had no weeds growing, only a multitude of footprints in the soft dirt.

Pilar took up her position and Ben stood opposite her. Ed and Christine set themselves on the north side of the circle. Sam and Lacey made up the south. When they were all in position, Ben bowed his head. They all did likewise, and made silent prayers to whatever powers that be.

Pilar had her brass vase, already populated with several sticks of incense. She struck a match and lit them one by one, her lips moving in silent invocation. Then she passed the matches to Sam, who passed them on down to Ben. He lit a smudge stick and blew on it gently until it began to smoke.

Pilar raised her incense and began to speak. She lifted the fragrant smoke to the east, to the west, to the north and south. Her voice was soft but firm, gentle but sure. She stepped forward, set her vase in the center of the circle, and took up her position again.

Ben's turn. He raised the smudge stick and acknowledged the four cardinal directions, his low Navajo words coming in a singsong voice. He raised his hands to the sky, then reached down toward the earth. He whispered to the fire within the smudge stick, and praised the wind that carried the smoke away. Then he, too, set the smudge stick in the center of the circle and stepped back.

They all joined hands. Lacey clutched Sam's tightly, but then noticed how gentle Ben's grip was, and she relaxed her hold on her partner.

"I love you, Sam," she whispered.

He flashed her a grin. "I love you, too, Lacey."

Lacey closed her eyes and breathed deeply, relaxing her body. She had already decided on one of the visualizations they'd discussed last night, and she worked now to construct the image in her mind. She imagined she could see the beating heart of each person here, the heart shining like a light from the center of the body. Each, she found, shone a slightly different color. Pilar's was bright white. Ben's was a brilliant gold. Sam's was royal blue. The colors pulsed with the heartbeats of each organ.

Da-DUM. Da-DUM. Da-DUM.

She breathed in the images, the colors, the heartbeats. Her body relaxed, all the tension draining away as she listened only to the combined beat of the many hearts.

Da-DUM. Da-DUM.

Something plucked at her hair, her shirt. The breeze freshened and gusted. At first she only noticed but thought nothing of it, but then it grew stronger. It tugged at her clothes, it blew a smattering of dirt into her eyes. Her body tightened involuntarily. She lost the heartbeat.

No, she thought, struggling to get the visualization back. *Think of nothing but love. Nothing but love.* She gripped Sam's hand tighter and imagined his love for her pouring into her. This love that she was so hesitant to accept. This love that he gave so freely. How could she doubt it? It was as strong as his fingers gripping hers, as bottomless as his dark eyes. She imagined all the colors of it glowing, growing stronger. His warm copper skin; his blue-black hair; the electric blue that pulsed from his heart. The heartbeat growing louder.

Da-DUM. Da-DUM.

The wind shrieked. It barreled around the corner of the house and slammed into the circle. Lacey felt it push against her back; she took a half step to widen her stance and anchor herself to the ground. Mother Earth. Source of all matter. A mother's love.

She gripped Sam's and Ben's hands more tightly. She imagined a steel rod up her spine, reaching down into the earth, keeping her strong, keeping her stable. Safe. The safety of Mother Earth. The love of the Mother. The love of the sphere of people around her. Her family.

A dust devil whirled up. Lacey couldn't see it, her eyes still tightly shut, but she could feel it. It shot granules of sand at her face, whipped her body, dragged her hair into a wild tangle. She ducked her head.

The wind howled. It blew up a cloud of dirt and grit and pelted the people with it. It slammed into them, first from one side, then the other. Lacey could hear a *foomp* as it smacked against the adobe wall of the house.

She desperately wanted to open her eyes, check all the men in the circle to make sure none of them were in distress, but she held off. If they were, they would make noise. If Sam were in trouble, she would know. She would know, even if she wasn't clinging to his hand. Their love connected them beyond the physical touch. It emanated from each of them, came together, combined, and flowed back into them. She would know. She turned her attention and her imagination back to the glowing hearts, the loving hearts. Hearts of white and gold and blue. Hearts pulsing with love, with life, with hope and kindness.

Da-DUM. Da-DUM.

The wind coiled around her like a snake, the force of it spiraling around her legs, her body, squeezing like a constrictor. She imagined the glow of her heart like a white light, cutting through the coils, but her chest began to feel tight, her throat closing up. She lifted her head and willed her body to breathe, to expand and relax, breathe in and out, in and out.

Da-DUM. Da-DUM.

The roar of the wind was like a blast in her ear, a demon screaming at her, the spittle from his enraged mouth speckling her face. She dared not wipe it away. In her mind she saw the face of it, twisted, howling, apoplectic with rage. She stood tall and lifted her face to the sun, the warm glowing sun, the heart of the universe, beating, beating.

Da-DUM. Da-DUM.

All the colors of the rainbow filtered down to her from the sun and melted against her eyelids. Warmed her in its loving light.

The wind tore at her. She kept her face lifted to the sun. The wind screamed. She imagined all the colors of love. The dust devil churned, pelting her with dirt and gravel. She felt the infusion of light from the sun expanding her heart.

A fierce blast slammed her. She felt something hard crash against her shin, the pain white hot, and wondered briefly if it had broken her leg. She clamped her jaws tight and held steady. The wind churned around her, between her feet, up her legs, squeezing her body, buffeting her head. It ripped the air away from the kerchief on her face; she couldn't breathe. It slashed and tore and screamed and shrieked. It pounded her, shook her, railed at her, all to no effect.

Impotent. Useless. A show of fury. Empty air.

And was gone.

The air settled. The dust fell back to the ground. The sounds faded away. The silence returned.

Lacey opened her eyes. The circle was complete. Everyone stood in their place. Disheveled, dirty, clothes askew, ears, eyes and hair caked with dirt. But alive and standing.

Love had won.

~~~

The cut on her leg wasn't bad. Pilar's vase had cracked the skin but not the bone. The old woman cleaned the wound and put a bandage over it while the rest of them walked the property.

"Well?" Lacey asked when they crowded into the living room.

"Gone," Sam said. "Clean."

Ben nodded, his leathery brown face split with a grin.

Lacey felt like they all breathed easier. As if the entire house exhaled in relief.

And maybe it did.

~~~

TWENTY-THREE

An almost full moon hung over the neighborhood. The night air was still, except for the occasional shout or scream of a titillated child.

Lacey and Sam stood on the sidewalk, holding hands. They watched Kenzie and her best friend Emily as they held out their trick-or-treat bags to the homeowners. An older woman oohed and aahed over their costumes. Emily was a *Frozen* ice princess. Kenzie was a witch.

Energized by their latest score, the two girls hurried back to their escorts.

"Snickers!" Kenzie reported.

"Next!" Emily headed for the next house on the block.

Sam and Lacey ambled along behind.

"Do you do this every year?" she asked.

"Pretty much. Last year I went with Daniel and his friends while Christine and Ed went with Kenzie. With Daniel thinking he's too old now, I guess we'll have to take turns."

Daniel, Lacey knew, was at home with his mom and stepdad, handing out goodies at the door. Practically an adult at thirteen.

"When's the last time you went trick-or-treating?" Sam asked.

"Hmm." Lacey calculated. "Twenty years ago? Maybe twenty-one. I don't know."

Didn't know and didn't care. She was feeling too content to even probe her brain for the answer.

As they reached the next house, Sam released her hand and slid his arm around her, pulling her close. She came willingly, resting her head against his shoulder. She sighed.

"Happy?" he asked.

"Yeah." She grinned at him. "There's something about banishing a demon that just feels very satisfying."

"Not to mention freeing tortured souls, giving an old woman some peace and saving a historic landmark from future liability," he added.

"Yeah, that, too," she agreed. Pilar had thanked them in her simple way with tea and hugs. The Mission San Juan Capistrano had been more monetarily inclined, pleasantly so. Sam had shared some of it with Ed, and offered some to Ben, but the old man refused. What did he need to buy?

"I hope all the excitement wasn't too hard on Ben," she said.

"I'm guessing he'll rest up for a few days, then go right back to making clay pots," he said. "I think the long drive was harder on him than the actual exorcism. I have a feeling he enjoyed being called in on this."

She nodded. "It was great to see him. We'll have to go out to the reservation in the not-too-distant future. I don't want too many months to go by before we see him again."

She paused. All this talk was prodding her toward a resolution she'd been forming in her mind. It seemed like the right time.

"Sam?"

"Hmm?"

"Do you remember, a while back, when you said that not trying was the same as failing?"

He leaned away from her slightly, inclining his head down toward her so he could look into her eyes. "Yes."

She pulled in a breath. "Well, I've been thinking. Thinking about all this, what we did. If we didn't try, we wouldn't have succeeded. If we didn't take the chance, nothing would have changed. But we did it, and it worked. Love worked." She tried to smile up at him, but her mouth quivered. "I think—no, I know—that I'm ready to take the next chance. I'm ready to go all in. I mean, if you still want me."

A slow smile curved his mouth. "*If* I still want you?" he asked. He brushed a strand of red hair off her forehead, then frowned thoughtfully. "Actually, though, after all the cases we've solved, all the challenges we've faced, all the times you saved me and I saved you, I was thinking there might be someone better suited for me, out there." He motioned out into the night with his chin. "I mean, there's a chance of that, right?"

She poked a rigid finger into his stomach. "No. There's no chance of that at all." She melted against him. "There's no one out there like me for you. And no one like you for me."

He pulled her close. "Does that mean you'll move in with me?"

She laughed. "Yes. Just as soon as you want me."

He took her wrist and checked her watch. "What time is it now?"

Just then her phone chimed. She pulled it out of her pocket and checked the screen.

"It's Carmen," she said in a surprised voice. "I should answer this." He nodded and she picked up the call. "Hi, Carmen."

"Lacey? I'm sorry to bother you, but I, uh, wanted to give you some news. I thought you'd want to know."

Lacey didn't like the sound of her voice. "What is it?" she asked with concern. "Is Pilar okay?"

Carmen hesitated. "Actually, no. She's gone."

"Gone?" Lacey glanced up at Sam.

"She died. Yesterday. There was a fire. The entire house burned down. She was inside. She didn't burn to death," Carmen rushed to add. "It was smoke inhalation."

"Oh, my God," Lacey breathed. "Carmen, I am so sorry. Oh, my God. I—I..."

"I know," Carmen said. "It's a shock, even though she had a good, long life."

"Do they know how the fire started?" she asked.

"They think it was a candle. Just a tragic accident. I mean, she had candles going all the time, and incense. But as old as she was, it's not surprising she might have forgotten about one."

"No," Lacey said. "Not at all." But she didn't believe that. Not for a minute. Pilar had set herself free. She had no more caretaking duties, so she had freed herself to go on to the next journey, whatever that was.

"Um, so what happens to the property?" she asked. "One of her children inherits it?" Even knowing the property was now clear, thinking of someone building a home on it made her nervous.

"Funny you should ask," Carmen said. "She left a will with my uncle. She wants the property turned into a park, with a memorial to her father and husband. She stipulates in the will that no structure other than the memorial ever be built on the property. Isn't that weird?"

Lacey looked up at Sam and smiled. "Actually, I don't think that's weird at all," she said. "I think that's a perfectly heavenly idea."

And she and Sam would be among the first to visit.

~~~

Thank You for Reading

I sincerely hope you enjoyed reading this book as much as I enjoyed writing it. If you did, I would greatly appreciate a short review on Amazon or your favorite book website. Reviews are crucial for any author, and even just a line or two can make a huge difference.

--MJB

ABOUT THE AUTHOR

Melissa Bowersock is an eclectic, award-winning author who writes in a variety of fiction and non-fiction genres: paranormal, action, romance, fantasy, spiritual, satire and biography. She lives in a small community in Northern Arizona with her husband and an Airedale terrier.

For more information, visit
http://www.newmoonrising.net
or
http://www.melissabowersock.com

Find Me Online on Twitter and Facebook or visit my blog at:

http://mjb-wordlovers.blogspot.com

BOOKS BY MELISSA BOWERSOCK

The Appaloosa Connection (Western Adventure)

When Ross Garvey's prized Appaloosa is stolen from his Colorado ranch, he fully intends to hunt down the thieves in their New Mexico hideout and regain his best broodmare. What he doesn't count on is bull-headed, fifteen year old Jaimie Callahan, whose horse was also stolen by the same thieves. And he certainly does not anticipate the beautiful Mexican girl who's dealing with the thieves, nor the fact that an entire company of Mexican troops is in on the deal!

The Blue Crystal (Fantasy)

In the realm of Zor, the tyrant Mal-Zor is maniacal in his quest for the mythical Blue Crystal of power sends generations of innocents to their deaths in the crystal mines. Jared, a young farmer from a small isolated village, has paid scant attention to the distant troubles until his younger siblings are taken as slaves. Jared vows to free them and his quest soon becomes enmeshed in the most magical power struggle imaginable. Accompanied by a recalcitrant halfling, mounted on a huge black lion and supported by an aging wizard and his daughter, Jared prepares to challenge the king and claim his hidden destiny.

Burning Through (Paranormal Suspense/Romance)

When Jennifer and Robert Stinson buy a beautifully restored Victorian house, the last thing they expect is to share their home with a ghost—especially one with a penchant for setting fires. Unfortunately the ghostly arson only creates more tension in their already strained marriage. Jen launches her own investigation into the history of her house and discovers a surprising ally in a sympathetic fire captain. But can she unravel the mystery of the fires before they consume her home, her marriage … and her life?

The Field Where I Died (Paranormal)

Devon Muir has always been fascinated with the Civil War. When he discovers that his fourth great-grandfather fought at pivotal battles like Antietam and Gettysburg, he is compelled to follow in his ancestor's footsteps and experience the battlefields on his own. What he doesn't count on is dreaming about a battle every night—and being killed every time. Now his exploration of battlefields becomes a different kind of quest as he struggles to understand who is the soldier he becomes in his dream, and who is the woman whose face he sees as he lays dying.

Finding Travis – **No Time for Travis: Book 1 (Time Travel)**

Travis Merrill's life isn't going according to plan. He's quit several career paths, his wife has left him, and his only solace is volunteering to portray a cavalry surgeon at historic Fort Verde in Arizona, a place where time seems to stand still. When a weird trick of time actually sends him back to the year 1877, he's boxed into impersonating the post surgeon for real. Unfortunately, he finds his medical knowledge is no match for the primitive practices of the day, and he's forced to make life or death decisions, not always successfully. He wonders if he will ever be able to return to his own time, or if he might find a life—and a love—140 years in the past.

Being Travis – No Time for Travis: Book 2 (Time Travel)

Two years ago, a weird trick of time sent Travis Merrill spiraling from 2016 to the year 1877. Committed now to his life in frontier Arizona, Travis is married with a child on the way and is homesteading a ranch. His knowledge of the future, however, keeps him at odds with his neighbors, his friends... and his wife. He finds it more and more difficult to protect his home without alienating his family, yet he can't ignore what he knows is – and will be – true.

Fleischerhaus (Paranormal Suspense/Romance)

Julia Martin, newly-divorced but still reeling from her husband's infidelity, takes a much needed vacation to visit old college friends in Germany. While touring a little-known concentration camp and museum, she spontaneously experiences a violent past life memory of being murdered in this very camp during the Holocaust. Efforts to understand her memories only lead to more questions, the largest being: is her killer still alive? Supported by her friends and comforted in the arms of a handsome doctor, Julia strives to uncover the mysteries of her past life and find justice for the person she used to be.

*Ghost Walk (*Paranormal Mystery)
A Lacey Fitzpatrick and Sam Firecloud Mystery Book 1

Lacey Fitzpatrick is an ex-LAPD detective with an axe to grind. Tainted by the betrayal of her drug-dealing cop boyfriend, she's on a quest to prove to herself—and the world—that she's still a competent crime-fighter. In order to do that, she teams up with Sam Firecloud, a half-Navajo man who communicates with ghosts. With his talent and her research, they tackle troubling unsolved crimes, but their latest case is the toughest. They have to solve a murder—where no record of a murder even exists. Can Sam glean enough information from the victim's ghost to unravel the mystery, and can Lacey convince the authorities that the murder actually happened?

***Skin Walk* (Paranormal Mystery)**
A Lacey Fitzpatrick and Sam Firecloud Mystery Book 2

Lacey and Sam are on the job again. This time, the ex-cop and the Navajo medium have been called out to the Navajo reservation to investigate the suspicious death of Sam's cousin. What they uncover leads them into a realm of the supernatural beyond anything Lacey ever imagined; her years on the LAPD did nothing to prepare her for dealing with witches and shapeshifters. With clues few and far between, can they determine who the murderer is before they themselves become the target of deadly curses and feral shapeshifter beasts?

Star Walk (**Paranormal Mystery***)*
A Lacey Fitzpatrick and Sam Firecloud Mystery Book 3

Ex-cop Lacey Fitzpatrick and Navajo medium Sam Firecloud are working a new investigation into paranormal activity. This time they're called to clear an old Hollywood mansion of the multiple ghostly tenants that are threatening the home owner's livelihood. At the same time, however, Lacey gets a call from her ex-boyfriend, now prison inmate, for help in a more earthly manner. He fears his sister is siphoning money from his elderly mother, and only Lacey can find out the truth. Between saving her ex's mother from bankruptcy and researching deep into the families of the tortured souls haunting the mansion, Lacey finds the revelations of family dynamics to be both fatally flawed and heartbreakingly inspired.

***Dream Walk* (Paranormal Mystery)**
A Lacey Fitzpatrick and Sam Firecloud Mystery Book 4

Private investigator Lacey Fitzpatrick and Navajo medium Sam Firecloud are usually called to clear haunted locations of their lingering ghosts using Sam's unusual talent for communicating with the dead. This time, however, the dead—Sam's former brother-in-law—comes to him… in a dream. Now Sam and Lacey have to go to Las Vegas and figure out how to find the body and uncover a murder plot before the murderers bury them forever.

***Dragon Walk* (Paranormal Mystery)**
A Lacey Fitzpatrick and Sam Firecloud Mystery Book 5

Four months ago, a pretty young marathoner disappeared while training on the isolated trails of Griffith Park in Los Angeles. The police have few leads, no witnesses and no results. As a last resort, they call in private investigator Lacey Fitzpatrick and Navajo medium Sam Firecloud to pick up the rapidly cooling trail. Sam and Lacey, however, are on the outs. Their efforts to take their relationship to the next level failed miserably, and now they must redefine their working relationship, as well. Can they find the murdered girl and her killer, and still hang on to their partnership?

***Demon Walk* (Paranormal Mystery)**
A Lacey Fitzpatrick and Sam Firecloud Mystery Book 6

Private investigator Lacey Fitzpatrick and Navajo medium Sam Firecloud are called in by the Director of Mission San Juan Capistrano to unravel the mystery surrounding an evil presence that is threatening the mission's people and its liability, maybe its very existence. While Lacey digs into the research, Sam pulls out all the stops, planning to fight fire with fire and witchcraft with… witchcraft. Lacey finds his methods disturbing, but knows they have to combat the ancient, supernatural force that has killed before, and may very well kill again.

***Soul Walk* (Paranormal Mystery)**
A Lacey Fitzpatrick and Sam Firecloud Mystery Book 7

Paranormal investigator Lacey Fitzpatrick and medium Sam Firecloud are making quite a name for themselves. When a TV network offers to feature them on a popular ghost series, they realize they could dispel misconceptions and bring credibility to their work. However, filming their process is more troublesome and complicated than they know. Their goal to research and release the ghostly tenants of a haunted bed and breakfast in Malibu is at odds with the studio's penchant for sensationalism. On top of that, Sam finds his connection to one of the ghosts to be painfully personal, and he and Lacey struggle to keep their work, their relationship and their newfound stardom from unraveling.

***Blood Walk* (Paranormal Mystery)**
A Lacey Fitzpatrick and Sam Firecloud Mystery Book 8

The paranormal investigation team of Lacey Fitzpatrick and medium Sam Firecloud is keeping tabs on a serial killer case that's baffling the LAPD: four murders in a month, with no solid leads or suspects. When Sam and Lacey offer their assistance, the PD reluctantly agrees, but Sam gets more than he bargains for when he visits the crime scenes. In addition to picking up impressions from the victims, he's also receiving feelings from the killer himself. Sam's unusual connection to the murderer's mind may help them catch the criminal, but it could also lead the murderer to them. In a deadly race against time, Sam and Lacey piece the clues together to catch the killer before he catches them.

***Castle Walk* (Paranormal Mystery)**
A Lacey Fitzpatrick and Sam Firecloud Mystery Book 9

Paranormal investigators Lacey Fitzpatrick and medium Sam Firecloud discover their reputation has spread around the world when they get a surprise call to investigate ghosts in an Irish castle. They're even more surprised when they learn it's the Castle Fitzpatrick, the ancestral home of the Fitzpatrick name, and Lacey's hopeful she can uncover some of her own family's history. But while they're researching that and the ghosts that Sam's walk has revealed, they get unexpected resistance from the castle owners. If Sam is wrong about the impressions he's received from the spirits, the releasement won't work, and the ghosts will be doomed to walk the castle forever.

*Murder Walk (*Paranormal Mystery*)*
A Lacey Fitzpatrick and Sam Firecloud Mystery Book 10

The best friend of Sam Firecloud's son, Daniel, has been murdered. The boy is having a hard enough time dealing with the loss but then discovers that he's inherited his father's mediumistic "gift" for communicating with the dead, a gift he doesn't want. Lacey Fitzpatrick, Sam's wife and partner, wants to start their own investigation into the murder, Sam is more worried about his son than the unsolved case, and Daniel just wants all ghosts to leave him alone. The family is being torn in three separate directions, but the murderer is still on the loose and may come after Daniel next, because the ghost is talking.

*Spirit Walk (*Paranormal Mystery*)*
A Lacey Fitzpatrick and Sam Firecloud Mystery Book 11

On the Navajo reservation, a man is found dead at the bottom of a canyon. The tribal police have ruled it an accident. People close to the man don't believe it, so medium Sam Firecloud and his partner, Lacey Fitzpatrick, are called in to investigate. When Sam's psychic "walk" confirms the worst fears, the clues lead him and Lacey forward, but the twisted path to the truth turns deadly when it seems the earth itself is trying to kill them.

*Fire Walk (*Paranormal Mystery*)*
A Lacey Fitzpatrick and Sam Firecloud Mystery Book 12

There's a property in the town of Meadeview, Massachusetts that has a problem with fire. Anything that is built there gets burned to the ground. Medium Sam Firecloud and his partner, Lacey Fitzpatrick, are called to the small town to investigate the strange physical haunting, and their research leads them deeper into the dark underbelly of the town. The more they

uncover, however, the more the townspeople are threatened by the old secrets—secrets they'd much rather see remain buried.

***Revenge Walk* (Paranormal Mystery)**
A Lacey Fitzpatrick and Sam Firecloud Mystery Book 13

Paranormal investigators Sam Firecloud and Lacey Fitzpatrick are preparing for a new venture—launching Sam's ceramic art studio with an open house. Their plans are suddenly derailed when someone targets Sam with deadly intent. The LAPD are on it, but leads are slim, and meanwhile they have a new haunting to research, one that is threatening small children. Neither investigation gives up clues easily, but Sam and Lacey have to keep working both before someone ends up dead.

***Gangster Walk* (Paranormal Mystery)**
A Lacey Fitzpatrick and Sam Firecloud Mystery Book 14

Technical whiz kid Cameron Gregory is one of the richest men in America, but even all his millions can't relieve him of a menacing ghost. Only medium Sam Firecloud and his partner, Lacey Fitzpatrick, can do that. Hosted in Gregory's luxurious Hudson Valley mansion, the paranormal investigators expect this job to be a piece of cake, but no one expects their research to lead them into the mysterious disappearance of a mobster kingpin from almost a hundred years ago.

***Karma Walk* (Paranormal Mystery)**
A Lacey Fitzpatrick and Sam Firecloud Mystery Book 15

Abe Sydlowski was a cop in Long Beach, California, and had a long, distinguished career—until he died. Now his ghost is appearing at a beach he used to patrol, and his brothers of the shield want to know why. Lacey Fitzpatrick and medium Sam Firecloud are called in but get one surprise before they even start. Daniel, Sam's fourteen-year-old son, wants to work with them. When the trio goes to investigate, they find not one ghost, but two. Who is the young girl whose spirit haunts the beach with Abe, and what's the connection between the two?

***Mystery Walk* (Paranormal Mystery)**
A Lacey Fitzpatrick and Sam Firecloud Mystery Book 16

When paranormal investigators Lacey Fitzpatrick and Sam Firecloud are on a case, they are all in, and don't rest until the haunting is resolved. Now they've been invited to a Murder Mystery Weekend of role-play, sleuthing and fun. Lacey thinks they'll have an advantage because they're such practiced investigators, and the tangled trail of clues, motives and red herrings creates a fierce competition to find whodunit. Lacey fully intends to solve the mystery and win the prize, but the weekend turns out to be surprisingly different on very many levels.

***Bordello Walk* (Paranormal Mystery)**
A Lacey Fitzpatrick and Sam Firecloud Mystery Book 17

Jerome, Arizona, is known as the most haunted town in the state. In its history as an old west mining town, it endured explosions, cave-ins, fires, and the usual consequences of rampant prostitution, gambling and gunfights. It experienced enough mayhem to generate countless ghosts, which is exactly why medium Sam Firecloud does not want to go there. When he and partner Lacey Fitzpatrick get a call to eradicate a ghost from an old bordello, there's more at stake than simply freeing a tortured soul. Sam's own soul could also be in danger.

***Storm Walk* (Paranormal Mystery)**
A Lacey Fitzpatrick and Sam Firecloud Mystery Book 18

Los Angeles has been besieged with relentless rain for weeks. There have been massive flooding, swift-water rescues, and an entire warehouse has collapsed from the weight of catastrophic rainfall, resulting in the death of six people. When medium Sam Firecloud is asked to connect with the only "witnesses"—the victims—he finds more questions than answers. He and his partner, Lacey Fitzpatrick, must take on the police, the insurance company and the architectural firm as they realize that things are not as they seem. Sam and Lacey aren't experts in any of the associated fields, but they do know one thing—the dead don't lie.

***Predator Walk* (Paranormal Mystery)**
A Lacey Fitzpatrick and Sam Firecloud Mystery Book 19

When medium Sam Firecloud and his partner, paranormal investigator Lacey Fitzpatrick, are called in on a new case, it appears to be a normal haunting, if there is such a thing. But neither is prepared for the effect this ghost has on Lacey, nor the ripple effect through their own relationship. Suddenly it's not just sending a lost spirit on its way that concerns them, but Lacey's own mental and emotional health, and—perhaps—the future of their partnership.

***Prayer Walk* (Paranormal Mystery)**
A Lacey Fitzpatrick and Sam Firecloud Mystery Book 20

Based in sprawling Los Angeles, medium Sam Firecloud and his partner, Lacey Fitzpatrick, never seem to run out of hauntings to investigate and resolve, but when they get two separate calls from two frantic customers, they realize they're getting stretched pretty thin. How are they going to handle two cases at once? Daniel,

Sam's fifteen-year-old son, has a solution, but they quickly discover that solution could lead to serious injury—or worse—for the supernaturally talented boy.

Mind Walk (Paranormal Mystery)
A Lacey Fitzpatrick and Sam Firecloud Mystery Book 21

Sam Firecloud's job as a medium is pretty straightforward: along with his partner, Lacy Fitzpatrick, he investigates hauntings, researches the ghosts to find out what keeps them tethered to the earth plane, and he releases them. But a new call for assistance brings a surprising request: a neurologist wants to study Sam's brain as he's connecting with lost spirits. The study is one thing, but when Sam and Lacey look deeper, they soon realize the doctor has a hidden agenda, and it's not scientific at all.

Deception Walk (Paranormal Mystery)
A Lacey Fitzpatrick and Sam Firecloud Mystery Book 22

The paranormal investigative duo of Lacey Fitzpatrick and Sam Firecloud are doing fine, but when an ex-girlfriend of Sam's shows up, Lacey feels uneasy. Sam has never talked much about his past, so the sudden arrival of a beautiful blonde is disturbing. However, when that same blonde disappears without a trace, and Sam is the last person to see her, Lacey realizes her worries are just beginning. The LA County Sheriff's office and the LAPD know more than they're saying—and they both consider Sam a suspect.

***Innocent Walk* (Paranormal Mystery)**
A Lacey Fitzpatrick and Sam Firecloud Mystery Book 23

Lacey Fitzpatrick and Sam Firecloud know that Kenzie, Sam's eleven-year-old daughter, has inherited his mediumistic abilities. The duo has tried to shelter Kenzie from the emotional and physical violence that often accompany their cases, but when a school bus crashes directly in front of Lacey and Kenzie, the girl is plunged into the heart of the tragedy. Some children survive, but many don't. Kenzie wants to help both the living and the dead, but some selfish and self-centered adults threaten the process.

Can Kenzie free the young, trapped souls, or are the children doomed to purgatory?

***Monster Walk* (Paranormal Mystery)**
A Lacey Fitzpatrick and Sam Firecloud Mystery Book 24

Two recent murders have rocked the small town of Chinle, Arizona, on the Navajo Reservation. Navajo Tribal Police have found no connection between the victims even though both were killed the same way and brutally mutilated. Lieutenant John Stoneburner has no choice but to call in medium Sam Firecloud and his partner, Lacey Fitzpatrick, to see if they can make sense of the grisly facts. When it becomes clear to Sam that the murders are related to ancient Navajo mythology, he enlists the help of an elder, his grandfather Ben, who leads them all into the perilous realm of gods and monsters.

***Dead Sea Walk* (Paranormal Mystery)**
A Lacey Fitzpatrick and Sam Firecloud Mystery Book 25

In 1947, the first Dead Sea scrolls—parchment containing 2,000-year-old versions of Biblical text—were discovered in caves above Qumran, Israel. Archaeological study of Qumran suggests it was a community of Essenes, ascetic monks whose teachings influenced the earliest Christian thought. When medium Sam Firecloud is invited to walk the ruins to connect with a spirit there, he wonders what—or who—he'll find. The executive director of Qumran has a guess; he believes the soul who dwells there could be no less than the ghost of Jesus Christ.

Heart Walk (**Paranormal Mystery**)
A Lacey Fitzpatrick and Sam Firecloud Mystery Book 26

In an older LA neighborhood, a nearly eighty-year-old house is haunted by a very persistent—and threatening—ghost. Multiple efforts to convince the ghost to move on have failed. When medium Sam Firecloud and his partner Lacey Fitzpatrick are called in to take a stab at it, they quickly realize there is more to the story than they know. The only question is, can they unravel the mystery before the enraged ghost takes out its revenge… on them?

*Night Walk (*Paranormal Mystery*)*
A Lacey Fitzpatrick and Sam Firecloud Mystery Book 27

When medium Sam Firecloud first hears about an Amber Alert on the Navajo reservation, he is stunned to realize the missing girl is his own young cousin. He and his partner, Lacey Fitzpatrick, rush to the scene in an attempt to help find the girl, aided by Sam's grandfather Ben. When the Fireclouds are dismissed by the FBI agents that are working the case by standard means, Sam takes measures into his own hands, and finds the pathway before him leads into the depths of the supernatural… and death.

*Stone Walk (*Paranormal Mystery*)*
A Lacey Fitzpatrick and Sam Firecloud Mystery Book 28

Who knew there was a Scottish castle hiding on a high promontory over Monterey, California? Lacey Fitzpatrick and medium Sam Firecloud certainly didn't; not until they were called in to investigate ghostly manifestations. The Gold Rush-era castle is being restored as a museum, but the most important plans have been derailed due to the refusal of frightened workers to trespass onto the outraged spirit's territory. When Sam and Lacey attempt to unravel the truth behind the angry ghost, they are plunged into a grisly, hidden culture of unspeakable rituals.

*Execution Walk (*Paranormal Mystery*)*
A Lacey Fitzpatrick and Sam Firecloud Mystery Book 29

On a lazy morning, paranormal investigators Sam Firecloud and Lacey Fitzpatrick take some rare time off and head for the beach—Huntington Beach, to be exact. What they don't expect is to wander onto the scene of a brutal murder committed the night before. When Sam's initial impressions are surreptitiously recorded by TV cameras at the same time that a local psychic named Anubis makes startling claims about the murder, news journalists smell a ratings bonanza—the battle of the psychics. All Sam and Lacey want to do is stop the killer from killing again, which turns out to be more complex than they'd imagined—

especially with the annoying distraction of being partnered with Anubis.

*Suicide Walk (*Paranormal Mystery*)*
A Lacey Fitzpatrick and Sam Firecloud Mystery Book 30

Raising teenagers is tough. Medium Sam Firecloud and his partner, Lacey Fitzpatrick, have that brought home to them in spades when Sam's sixteen-year-old son, Daniel, calls a sudden family meeting to make an unexpected, and unwelcome, announcement. Not only are Sam and Lacey struggling to deal with the development, they're doing it in different ways, adding to the tension. At the same time, they are hired to investigate the death of a fifteen-year-old girl who chose to tragically end what was a privileged but tragic life. When Sam's usual methods for dealing with a tethered soul go stunningly wrong, he and Lacey are left to wonder if they can ultimately help either of the two teens—living and dead—to find peace.

*Twilight Walk (*Paranormal Mystery*)*
A Lacey Fitzpatrick and Sam Firecloud Mystery Book 31

Paranormal investigators Lacey Fitzpatrick and Sam Firecloud have their lives turned upside down by a sudden medical emergency that sidelines Lacey for the foreseeable future. At the same time, however, the LAPD is stymied by what appears to be a serial murderer, and not just the ordinary garden variety. This one leaves teeth marks on the victims' necks. Is a vampire loose in LA? Sam intends to find out, and must plunge alone into the dark underground of bloodlust culture. Can he track down the evidence by himself, and can recalcitrant Lacey follow doctor's orders long enough to let her body heal?

*Redemption Walk (*Paranormal Mystery*)*
A Lacey Fitzpatrick and Sam Firecloud Mystery Book 32

When medium Sam Firecloud and his partner, Lacey Fitzpatrick, are called in to investigate a haunting, they find out very quickly that the spirit is their client's mother—and she is a poltergeist. The recently departed soul moves random objects around the house, seemingly without purpose. Sam knows the ghost has a story to tell, but it's hidden deep in the past. Although the secret threatens to tear the family apart, if Sam and Lacey can't figure out the clues and uncover the whole truth, the ghost will be bound in agony to the earth plane—forever.

*Hopi Walk (*Paranormal Mystery*)*
A Lacey Fitzpatrick and Sam Firecloud Mystery Book 33

Navajo police officer John Stoneburner is a tough cookie who hates to rely on anyone else, especially Sam Firecloud with his "woo-woo" abilities. So when John asks Sam to investigate the death of his own brother, Sam knows John is totally out of ideas. The investigation centers on Blue Canyon, a scenic and spiritual area of the Hopi reservation. When Sam walks the location, he not only connects with John's brother, but also with other enraged spirits that are out for revenge, and that don't care who they exact it from.

Healing Walk *(Paranormal Mystery)*
A Lacey Fitzpatrick and Sam Firecloud Mystery Book 34

Medium Sam Firecloud and his investigative partner, Lacey Fitzpatrick, are used to being called in to rid homes of ghosts, but are surprised when they're asked to investigate a haunting in a hospital. The case turns out to be more difficult than usual for two reasons: the ghost doesn't actually understand what caused the death, and the administrator of the hospital does not want the paranormal pair and their unorthodox methods connected to his facility in any way. Sam and Lacey are determined to find out the information they need to release the ghost, but can they do it before the administrator makes good on his threats to have them thrown in jail?

Trojan Walk **(Paranormal Mystery)**
A Lacey Fitzpatrick and Sam Firecloud Mystery Book 35

Sweltering under the summer heat of LA in July, Lacey Fitzpatrick begins planning an Alaskan cruise getaway for herself and her partner Sam, but her efforts are being constantly interrupted by annoying phone calls. Whoever it is, the person calls, says nothing, and hangs up. Then Sam starts getting the same kind of calls. The first possibility the duo considers is that some criminal they helped incarcerate is purposely irritating them or taking out a petty revenge, but after doing a bit of research, Lacey discovers that the caller—and the reason for the calls—is far more disturbing and complex. Now the question is, can the paranormal investigators really do anything to help?

*Betrayal Walk (*Paranormal Mystery*)*
A Lacey Fitzpatrick and Sam Firecloud Mystery Book 36

When Sam and Lacey are called to what was an abandoned house outside Houston, Texas, Lacey's research reveals what looks like a well-documented and straightforward case. Armed with extensive information, they plan to release the ghost, but there's only one hitch: if what they've found is true, why is the ghost so enraged? And will anything placate the spirit so it can move on?

Goddess Rising **(Spiritual Fantasy)**

It is the future, and a global geologic holocaust has destroyed civilization, leaving only a tiny fraction of people to rebuild scattered colonies. Reduced to a primitive state, they live close to the earth and cultivate a Goddess worship, and chosen ones dream a prophecy that Greer, a female savior, will return them to greatness. An epic and magical story of one woman's exceptional destiny during exceptional times, *Goddess Rising* follows Greer's journey from simple obscurity to prophesied reign. Acknowledged as the face of the Goddess on earth, Greer discovers the rewards of power—and its price—as she struggles through her own labyrinth of fear and desire, sexuality and sacrifice, love and death.

Lightning Strikes **(Contemporary Romance)**

Jessie Evans is a free-lance journalist, emphasis on the "free," with no plans to tie herself down. While researching a story in Flagstaff about Indian influences in Arizona, however, she encounters Lucas Shay, a smoldering paradox who is part Indian, part architect and all man. Whether igniting her temper with his arrogance or challenging her beliefs with his laser-like insight, Jessie can't deny that Lucas sets fire to her soul as well.

Love's Savage Armpit by Amber Flame (Satire) (Originally published as *The Pits of Passion*)

Sealed to the man in an arranged marriage, Elizabeth rides the surging tide of shock and denial, lust and love, as she is swept from the manicured gardens of England to the savage shores of Africa and the wilds of the New World, never quite sure which Captain Elliott is the man she loves. Warning! This satiric romp is NOT your mother's romance novel!

The Man in the Black Hat (Time Travel)

Clay Bauer, at the age of 38, is a second-rate actor in Hollywood. He's too mean-looking to get leading man roles in movies, so he's resigned himself to playing only villains.

While filming a low-budget Western in the red rocks of Sedona, Arizona, he hears about the vortices there — places of power where people claim to have strange experiences, even traveling to other dimensions. He doesn't believe any of it — until he accidentally passes through a vortex and is transported more than 100 years into the past. Suddenly he's faced with playing the most important role of his life. Only this time, it's for real.

Marcia Gates: Angel of Bataan **(Biography)**

Marcia L. Gates was an Army nurse and prisoner of war during WWII. As an "Angel of Bataan," she spent three years in a Japanese internment camp in the Philippines. This is her award-winning story, told through her letters and the newspaper clippings, photos and letters collected by her mother. The book was awarded a medal for biography by both the Military Writers Society of America and Stars and Flags.com and won honorable mentions at the Hollywood Book Festival and the Great Midwest Book Festival. It was featured in the documentary *Our Wisconsin: The Military History of America's Dairyland* produced by WKOW-TV in Madison.

The Rare Breed (Historical Romance)

The daughter of a white woman and an Indian brave, Catherine Boudry had spent the first thirteen years of her life among the Cheyenne. Restored at last to her mother's wealthy parents, Cathy blossomed into womanhood surrounded by all the "civilized" comforts of the white man's world. But at the age of twenty, the lure of her Indian heritage drew her back to the western plains. It was a journey that would awaken her to the joy and agony of passion in the arms of two very different men—Jory, the virile young trapper, and Barred Owl, the Cheyenne brave to whom she had been pledged in marriage long ago.

Remember Me (Contemporary Romance)

Elly Cole wakes up bruised and battered in a hospital-and has no idea who she is or how she got there. Her brooding giant of a husband informs her that she had been fleeing with her lover who was killed in the car accident that left her injured, that she is pregnant with that lover's child and that she has nowhere else to go but home-with him. Struggling against the threat of her husband's dangerous rage and jealousy, Elly strives to regain her memory and reconstruct the life she left behind, wondering how she could ever have loved this man who hates her.

***Queen's Gold* (Action/Adventure)**

Hal Thompson is a pretty ordinary guy. A widower who owns his own small business, he's doing his best to raise his two nearly adult children alone. When they convince him to undergo a hypnotic past-life regression, he is unimpressed that his "memories" reveal the hiding place of ancient Aztec gold. Other people, however, take it very seriously and when his family is threatened, he is forced to plunge into the jungles of Mexico, battling treacherous terrain, lethal wildlife and the haunting feeling of a love that spans centuries. Can he find the gold before it claims more lives? Or will he lose the love of his life ... again?

Sonnets for Heidi (Contemporary)

Trish Munroe never planned to be a caregiver, but circumstances have conspired to make her responsible for her elderly Aunt Heidi. Trish does her best to balance the demands of her job, her love life and Heidi's advancing Alzheimer's, but the pressure is taking its toll. When Heidi passes away, there's a bittersweet reprieve until Trish uncovers a family secret of forbidden love that takes her on a tragic yet triumphant journey of the heart.

Stone's Ghost **(Paranormal)**

Matthew Stone doesn't believe in ghosts ... until he meets one. He owns a successful business in Lake Havasu, Arizona, home to the famed London Bridge that was brought over stone by stone and rebuilt over the Colorado River. He has a gorgeous girlfriend, a doting mother, and more money than he needs, but no time for stories about the ghosts who were transplanted from England with the famed bridge. When a chance encounter with a female ghost leads to unexpected friendship, Matt and the ghost are forced to rely on each other as they confront the pasts that haunt them.

Superstition Gold (Historical Romance)

Married and widowed within a 24-hour period, beautiful Leigh Banning watches as her storybook New Orleans life crumbles away piece by piece. In a heartbroken attempt to start over, she travels to the wilds of frontier Arizona in an effort to understand the father she never knew and is rewarded with gold from the legendary Lost Dutchman gold mine in the Superstition Mountains. The gold comes with a price tag, however—the murder of innocent people. Leigh's quest for justice leads her to a remote Apache camp in the company of a proud Pima Indian and a handsome cavalry officer. Torn between the fiery kisses of the Major and the respectful love of the Pima, Leigh joins forces with the Apaches to battle gold-hungry killers and in the process discovers her true self and her one true love.

Made in the USA
Columbia, SC
17 July 2024